MARY'S
Christmas
GOODBYE

LINDA BYLER

Good ✿ Books

New York, New York

MARY'S CHRISTMAS GOODBYE

Good Books books may be purchased in bulk at special discounts for sales promotion, corporate gifts, fund-raising, or educational purposes. Special editions can also be created to specifications. For details, contact the Special Sales Department, Good Books, 307 West 36th Street, 11th Floor, NewYork, NY 10018 or info@skyhorsepublishing.com.

Good Books is an imprint of Skyhorse Publishing, Inc.®, a Delaware corporation.

Visit our website at www.goodbooks.com.

10 9 8 7 6 5 4 3 2 1

Library of Congress Cataloging-in-Publication Data available on file.

ISBN: 978-1-68099-366-0
eBook ISBN: 978-1-68099-117-8

Cover design by Koechel Peterson & Associates, Inc., Minneapolis, Minnesota

Printed in Canada

Table of Contents

Chapter One

SHE STRAIGHTENED HER BACK, ONE HAND RUBBING the sore spot below her shoulder blade. Still seventh- and eighth-grade stories to correct, and it was already five o'clock.

The classroom was bathed in the early spring sunlight, a pale yellow glow that turned the white walls into a golden color, the children's artwork into brighter colors as well. Another month of school, and she'd be free for the summer, or at least as free as any single, thirty-year-old Amish old maid would ever be.

Mary Stoltzfus wrinkled her nose, hiding some of the freckles that lay splattered across it. She rubbed at the end of her nose as if to eliminate a few more freckles, then gave up, allowing a tremendous sneeze to rip through her head. "Whoo!" she said to herself. Mary was alone in the one-room Amish schoolhouse in Ronks, Pennsylvania.

She sat back, grabbed a Kleenex from the small, square box on her desk, and honked into it before tapping her desk absentmindedly with the cap of her red Bic pen. How many Bic pens had she emptied through the years? Twelve whole years of teaching Chestnut Run School. Well, all but one month to go in this school year. She'd started her first term at eighteen years of age, inexperienced, nervous, so young, her only goal to be a teacher, and a good one.

The love of the children kept her going through difficult times, the way it kept her going through the good times, too.

She was an experienced schoolteacher now. She was on the board of the teachers' class, who were asked to help young teachers and give advice, which was expected after you'd been teaching for a while. It was all right, she supposed, this prestige in the world of teachers, but certainly not what kept her going from year to year.

Before she knew it, the coming summer would end and she'd be back in the classroom with fresh yellow pencils sharpened, stacks of new tablets, and gleaming workbook covers shining in neat rows on top of the folding table. Boxes of pink erasers, bottles of Elmer's Glue, new rulers smelling of wood, it was all she knew and all she wanted.

She read Ben Beiler's story, then leaned back so far she almost tipped her desk chair, hurriedly righted herself, thumped both elbows on her desk, and snorted loudly. Now, Ben could do better than that. He should be ashamed. She scrawled a red C- across his paper, with the words, "Hey. Come on!" written below. He'd know what she meant.

This time of year, too many Lancaster County farm boys had spring fever. They wanted to ride the hay wagons or follow the plows with tin cans, picking up worms to go fishing, the sea gulls circling overhead. They thought of new colts and calves, baby goats, and squealing piglets.

Mary sighed and bit down on her pen so hard it hurt her teeth. Ah, she was tired. Her eyes felt like the plastic black and white ones you stuck on art projects, the eyeballs rolling around unattached. She needed to make an appointment at the optometrist. *Da owa dokta.* The eye doctor, as her aging father put it. He couldn't pronounce the fancy word, that was sure.

She got up, swiped her desktop with the hem of her black apron that was pinned around her slim waist, then gathered up her lunchbox and book bag. She let herself out the door and down the steps.

Her eyes surveyed the playground, looking for bits of paper or orange peels, anything the playground cleanup crew had overlooked. There was nothing. Good. She'd have to let the second-grade students know she appreciated them. She closed the schoolhouse gate behind her and set off on the fifteen-minute walk home.

An oncoming horse and buggy bore down on her, the horse's head held high in the manner of Saddlebreds. She waved at John King, the neighbor man, then stepped away from the roadside to allow a car to pass. It slowed to a crawl with its window lowered as a passenger aimed a small red phone at her face.

Mary shrugged. They'd love the finished product—a tired, red-haired schoolteacher wearing a crooked covering with less than clean strings tied beneath her chin. Good for them. They could label it Scary Schoolteacher. She grinned, picking up her pace.

"Hello!" she called, yanking the screen door open. No one at home. Well, that was nothing new.

Her parents were empty-nesters who loved going away, visiting, shopping, helping the "marrieds," as she put it.

The house was long and low with wide white siding, a black roof, and a porch along the front. Four round white pillars supported the roof. A white picket fence kept the household as isolated as possible from the never ceasing flow of cars, trucks, horses and buggies, scooters, and pedestrians.

Her mother's hibiscus, ornamental grasses, and shrubbery, as well as begonias and pink geraniums, made the small garden a haven of color in summer. She'd already planted a few petunias, saying they'd take the frost.

Mary's apartment, or "end," was to the right of her parents' part of the house. She lived comfortably with her own small kitchen and seating area all in one, along with a bathroom and nice-sized bedroom. It was all she needed with plenty of space for company.

Her walls were white throughout the whole apartment, with the doors and trim the same color. Her collection of various antiques and oak furniture set her taste apart. Mary was a little different, the marrieds said, nodding their heads knowingly. She hung curtains at her windows that they thought were plain ugly. She was just trying to be in style. No wonder she was still single. Without children, yet.

She put her book bag on the old wooden chair that had been her grandmother's, then went to the pedestal oak table to sift through her mail. Propane gas bill. A credit card offer. Time to renew her subscription to *National Geographic*.

All of the *Geographic*s went to school with her, with a few pages torn out if she chose to eliminate anything improper.

Hm. What was this?

She slipped a thumbnail beneath the seal on the envelope, then ripped the end of it, and extracted one page of tablet paper. Her brow scrunched into deep furrows, the red hair that escaped the dusting of the morning's hair spray, waving and quivering on her forehead.

What? Someone wanted her to teach school in. . . . Where? Maine? "MT?" No, that was Montana.

She leaned forward, thumped the heels of her gray Nikes down hard, and read it again.

"Dear Mary."

She blew out impatiently through her nose. How informal was that? They could have been a bit more businesslike and written, "To Mary Stoltzfus," or "To Whom It May Concern." Maybe that was over the top, but still.

It was a wonder he didn't sign, "Love, Arthur Bontrager." What in the world kind of name was Arthur? Was he even Amish? Did they call him Art or Artie? She'd heard of Bontragers and Weavers and Schlabachs, but they lived out in the western states mostly.

Well, Montana was west. Way west. The wild, wild way-out-yonder-clear-to-the-moon west.

Mary folded the letter, stuck it back in the torn envelope, and said out loud, "Sorry, Artie. No can do."

She went to the refrigerator and popped the top on a can of Diet Pepsi, took a long swallow, burped, and breathed, "Ah!"

Now for her Dagwood sandwich. She placed a roll right side up, lathered it with mustard on one side and mayonnaise on the other, then piled sweet

Lebanon bologna, leftover turkey, Swiss cheese, hard-boiled egg slices, pickles, onion slices, and green peppers on top. She heated a can of Campbell's tomato soup until it was at the boiling point, added saltines and applesauce to cool it, then sat down to her evening meal.

Teach school in Montana? Yeah, well, this is what happened after you accumulated twelve years of experience. Everyone took for granted that you could move thousands of miles away and straighten out the mess they'd created. No wonder the children were a problem. She bet anything not one of them wanted to live at the end of civilization. Bless their transplanted little hearts.

A slice of egg squeezed out of her mouth, slid down her chin, and landed on the clean linoleum. Bending, she picked it up and stuck it back into the towering sandwich, her mind on the handwriting in the letter. Not bad, for a man.

His English was better than some Amish men she'd known. How had they even found her address? Or even knew who she was?

"Dear Mary." Now that was personal.

She scraped out the last of the tomato soup, then lifted the lid of a small wooden box, broke off half of a chocolate Kit Kat bar, and chewed methodically.

No, she wouldn't go. It was too far away. Besides, they wore those stiff coverings that stuck so far out the back, and there she'd be with her soft, organdy, heart-shaped covering, her black apron pinned about her waist, standing out like an owl in a flock of pigeons. No, no thanks. I'll pass.

She heard the crunch of steel buggy wheels turn in the drive and saw her parents seated on the spring wagon. Mam's face was red from the brisk wind. Dat's black felt hat was smashed down as far as it would go, his white hair and beard sprouting out beneath it, his cheeks ruddy with good health.

Why the spring wagon? It was too chilly. Now Mam would come down with the pleurisy, moaning and groaning and carrying the hot water bottle around like a second skin. Aging parents were sometimes as much worry as a classroom of twenty-one children.

But, of course, the powerful magnet called "parents" drew Mary to their door a few minutes later. She plopped on the worn blue recliner with the pink crocheted afghan slung across its back. Her backward force lifted the end of the afghan, flinging it over her head and thoroughly messing up her hair and covering, which hadn't been too straight to begin with.

Impatiently, she lifted the offensive throw and flung it to the floor beside her. "Why do you insist on covering all your chairs with those things?" Mary snapped.

"Now." Mam was in her early seventies, thin, and for all anyone could tell, as fit as a fiddle, in Dat's words. Her hair was white, her skin gently folded into wrinkles that showed her friendly character. She always had a smile on her face, and her hands were willing to help with whatever task presented itself.

"Mam, look at this." Mary shoved the letter into her mother's hands. Mam raised her eyebrows in question, then sat down and began to read.

Mary knew what was forthcoming before it actually came out. "My, oh," Mam said, soft and low.

Dat entered the kitchen whistling, hung his hat on a peg in the adjoining mud room, then bent to wash his hands. Hand-washing was necessary after driving and unhitching a horse. The smell of leather, horse sweat, and animal hair mingled to give off a distinctive odor.

Wiping his hands on the brown towel, he turned to look at his daughter. "School over?"

That was what he always said. Of course school was over for the day, or she certainly would not be sitting there.

"Yup."

That's what she always said, too.

Cars and trucks whizzed past the house, the steady clopping of horses' hooves accompanying them. Mary and her parents never thought about the noise. It was as natural as breathing. They lived in the humming tourist area of Lancaster County, so they had learned to adjust to the constant stream of traffic. The hustle and bustle, the gawking visitors, was a way of life. Amid all of it, including the Sunday meetings in homes, the Amish culture prospered and grew, a quiet way that remained untouched.

"Here. Read this." Mam handed over the letter. Dat lowered himself heavily into a chair, read slowly, his mouth moving as he whispered the words to himself.

"Well."

"What should I do? I'm not going so far away to teach those children."

"Then why do you ask what you should do?"

Mary shrugged. "Habit."

Mam smiled. "Aaron, what shall we have for supper?"

Mary went home, finished correcting the papers she'd brought, and prepared tomorrow's German lesson. Leaning back in her chair, she raised both arms above her head and flexed her fingers toward the ceiling, her mouth opening in a yawn of gigantic proportion. Time to shower and go to bed.

But there she lay on her side with her hands scrunched up beneath her chin, eyes closed, perfectly ready to nod off, but completely unable to stop the mad dash of thoughts in her mind.

Montana was vast without a lot of people anywhere. Weren't there snowy peaks and mountain ranges and pine forests? There were lions and wild burros and rattlesnakes called sidewinders and huge, hairy tarantulas. Or were they in Arizona?

What kind of Amish people would name their boy Arthur? King Arthur of the Round Table in medieval

times, his armor clanking as his steed's hooves pounded the earth, was pretty distant from the Amish!

Those western people allowed bikes. She could
picture herself pedaling along a country road, the
smell of fresh pine branches in her nostrils, her skirts
flapping in the breeze.

Then there were the mountain lions. Un-huh.

She'd wait a few days, think about the invitation,
and sleep on it. She flipped on her back, sighed, and
envisioned a row of sheep leaping across an imagi-
nary fence, counting each one as they landed on their
front hooves.

Well, it was definitely no. She was a citified
Lancaster Countian, used to the comforts of home,
money, having things handy. She even owned one of
the newfangled electric clothes washers some genius
had converted to the compressed air system. No more
lifting wet, twisted clothes out of pounding, frothy
water and stuffing them through a squeaky wringer.

If she felt like eating at a nice restaurant, she could.
She could call a driver, the handy person who made a
living hauling Amish people to places too bustling—
with too many stoplights and lanes of fast-moving

traffic—for a horse and buggy to go. And that wasn't very far away, just right down along Route 30 where all the outlets, hotels, motels, and restaurants vied to accommodate the thousands of tourists who descended on the farmlands of Lancaster County.

What did people in Montana do for entertainment? Probably roast buffalo steaks on an outdoor fire. Or no, buffalo were in Wyoming. What did they roast? Leg of mountain lion?

She sat straight up, lifted her pillow and thumped it against the oak headboard, folded it in half, and flung her head back down. Ow. Now she had a mean crick in her neck.

She picked up her pillow by one corner and threw it across the room, flipped over on her stomach, turned her head to one side, and closed her eyes. Now she didn't know what to do with her hands, so she stuffed them under her waist. That didn't work, either.

Thoroughly disgruntled, she sat up, put her feet on the rug and heaved herself upright, went to the kitchen, found the flashlight, and aimed it at the old schoolhouse clock above the table. 11:30. Oh, no. Tomorrow was a school day.

She opened the cupboard door above the refrigerator, brought down the box of Wheaties, scooped a generous amount of sugar on top, added a dash of whole milk, and thumped them good with the back of her spoon, then lifted a big spoonful to her mouth.

That was the thing about Wheaties. You could load an awful big bunch of them on a spoon with a bit of maneuvering and get them all in your mouth at one time, which made them twice as delicious, same as a filled doughnut. Wheaties were just delicious, she decided again, carefully getting every whole wheat flake to her mouth, then lifting the bowl and draining the sugary milk in one swallow.

There. Back to bed.

She wondered what God thought. She wished she was a prophet or at least a good person like Abraham. God told him very sternly to get out of the house and into a land that he knew nothing about, and his seed would outnumber the sands of the sea, or words to that effect. He made it very plain.

God wasn't that close or that easy to understand. In fact, he often seemed elusive. But then he might not have too much time for cranky, red-haired old maids who tried pretty hard to get their own way in most circumstances.

None of this, "Yes, Charles." "No, Charles." "Whatever you think best, Charles" kind of thing for her. Look at Ma Ingalls, dragged all over the Dakotas and Wisconsin, or wherever. Ah, well.

Please then, God, if you think it's okay to let me know, would you? Show me, direct me. You know, though, that I'm happy right here, don't you?

A truck roared past, shifted gears, and churned to the top of the low grade. Mary thought they should outlaw loud trucks but didn't think it would happen in her lifetime.

She finally fell asleep and, when she did, dreamed that every grain of sand was red like her hair.

That whole week everything seemed to go flat. Even the sunlight was tainted. She noticed the cracks in the tile flooring, the dozens of black scuff marks made by the pupils' shoes. She was irritated at the old stubborn desk drawers and cried when she couldn't find the WD40 to grease them.

The two eighth grade boys rolled tablet paper into cigarettes and almost burned the privy down, which resulted in an evening visit to both sets of parents, a splitting headache, and a sour stomach for days afterward.

Black smoke fumed from smokestacks of unbelievably noisy trucks, and tourists gawked, almost causing accidents with their sudden stops.

Mary noticed the unkempt schoolyard and the boards that needed to be replaced on the board fence surrounding it. The plastic cups on the shelf by the water hydrant looked soiled and broken. She wanted to sweep them to the ground, put them in the trash or do something, just to get rid of them.

She decided she was afflicted with a severe case of discontent. Once you started thinking things would be more exciting on the other side of the fence, things definitely soured on this side. More and more, her thoughts turned to, "Oh, what in the world does it matter?" Or, she'd be humming along, thinking, "Go for it."

What if she went for it—whatever "it" was—and she was stuck in a stinking old cabin somewhere, committed to nine long months of teaching, and she hated everything about it?

One thing she knew—she could never dislike children. In her opinion, children were God's gift to an otherwise crazy world. They were innocent, eager, funny, and painfully shy. They put in so much honest effort and were lovable, endearing, sweet, forthright—oh, the list never stopped. She didn't mind not having children of her own. She had twenty-one who were under her supervision five days a week, and she loved them like her own.

Finally Mam said that it seemed as if Mary needed to go to Montana just to take care of her curiosity, if for nothing else, because she wasn't being happy or friendly. Mary's heart leaped, then plunged with a sickening thud. "I can't travel that far alone," she squeaked.

"Of course you can. It's perfectly safe these days. I'm sure Amtrak's security system rivals the airlines."

"What do you know about it?"

"Sister Mattie was thoroughly searched."

Mary laughed appreciatively. "What about you and Dat?"

"What about us? Ten marrieds living so close? I'm quite sure we shall survive, maybe even thrive."

Mam's eyes twinkled, but her mouth turned wobbly, turning down only a bit at the corners. "I'll take care of your African violets for you."

"Am I going, then?"

"I would say you should try it."

"What does Dat say?"

"He knew you'd go. Just come home for Christmas."

Chapter Two

AND HERE I AM, MARY THOUGHT. SWAYING AND swerving wildly on this speeding silver bullet, determined to show the rest of these passengers I am a seasoned traveler, a woman about town, completely at ease with every person on this train.

All she could think of was which person could be a bomber or a highjacker? Which one would be a terrorist, smart enough to outwit the security system? Definitely the foreign-looking youth with the pitiful attempt at growing a beard. She bet anything that huge backpack beside him contained a paint can full of nails, ready to blow them all over the state of Indiana.

Or the sour-looking individual wearing dark glasses, slumped in a corner, a questionable-looking apparatus on the floor.

Well, what about that kindly old lady with the crocheted afghan across her knees, clutching the black, gleaming pocketbook in a death grip with gloved hands? Suddenly she thought of Mam's afghan, the pink color almost identical to the one across the old lady's knees, and wondered wildly how to go about getting off a speeding train. She'd get off at the next stop and ride the return train home. She could do that.

She watched the young man out of the corner of her eye and decided he was not nervous at all for someone with an explosive device in his backpack. She decided straightaway, then, that this fear was from the devil, and God would not want her to waste her time sinking into these suspicious thoughts.

After the wait in Chicago, the scenery turned into Mary's first glimpse of endless prairie, so fascinating she never tired of it. She slept fitfully, as if the strange movement of the cars, as they were being pulled headlong through an alien, spooky world, were just about to be hurled through the vast galaxy.

But once the train actually reached the state of Montana, Mary forgot everything else except the view outside the window of the fast-moving car. She had read about the western states, turned the globe to find North America, and then traced towns and highways and rivers with her forefinger. She pulled down maps and showed the upper grades the great and intricate web of roadways, rivers, and mountains.

Nothing could have prepared her for this, however. The sky was a blue bowl covering an unbelievable landscape of hills and valleys, pine forests, and wildflowers. There were simply no houses anywhere for miles and miles and miles. Eagles soared as if they could spread their majestic wings and sail on forever, uninhibited or untroubled by industry, towns, traffic, and any trace of human beings.

Sometimes Mary thought the word "awesome" was overused, overextended among the schoolchildren, but here there was no other word suitable.

They passed Billings, then towns called Cascade and Antelope, but finally, Mary realized, her destination was only half an hour away. She lurched to the restroom to check her appearance, aghast to find her face chalk-white, the freckles in stark contrast as if someone had thrown a handful of mud and some of it stuck. And her green eyes, ugh.

Mary turned away. She wasn't here in Montana for a beauty contest. She was here to exercise her expertise at teaching school. It was all she had.

I may not be much to look at, but I can turn your school into an efficient learning machine, I know it.

Where the train slid to a stop, the neat brown sign said only Loma, nothing else. No population count, barely even an acknowledgment of life except for the rickety shack they called a train stop. With knees turned to jelly, her fingers shaking as she pulled out the handle of her luggage, she made her way down the steps, thanking the concerned attendant, then stood in the loose gravel and dusty weeds, thinking that if she survived the next few hours, she'd be able to survive anything.

The sun was surprisingly warm. She lifted her face to it, marveling at the ability of the sun to shine here in this forsaken place, the same time as it shone thousands of miles—well, a thousand and hundreds—away on Lancaster County.

She stood perfectly still, her hands gripping the pull-out handle on her luxurious baggage from the outlet store. Royal blue, trimmed in black, from Coach. Well, she was fairly certain no one in Montana knew the label, but here she was. Probably should have thrown her things in a green, reusable, Food Lion grocery bag.

Wind puffed up the dust, throwing a few fine grains in her eyes. She turned her back to it, rubbed her eyes, and sneezed. A few grayish-green weeds were tossed about, looking tired and sick here by the railroad tracks.

Mary craned her neck, searching for any sign of life, and decided she was the sole occupant of the state of Montana. She may as well plant her flag, the way the Mount Everest guys did. She was hungry and thirsty, so she turned toward the graying little house that served as a station. A few tall skinny pines stood behind it, as if to keep it from blowing off into the wide sky. Grasping the loose doorknob, she twisted to the left, then the right, before it swung open, revealing a dusty little room containing a wooden bench, one metal folding chair, a torn cardboard box, and two half-dead mice.

Well, one thing sure, she wouldn't starve. She could always light a fire with the cardboard and roast the mice on a spit. No Pepsi machine. No water.

She scraped the palm of her hand across the rustic bench to clean off the dust, jumped, and smacked her hand against her cheek. Ow. A splinter.

And that is where Arthur Bontrager, the school board member, found the teacher from Pennsylvania —at the window, her back turned, her head bent, earnestly digging at the palm of her hand with a straight pin.

"Hey!"

Mary jumped, emitting a low, unladylike squawk.

"Didn't mean to scare you."

Hiding the pin, the splinter, the pain, and frustration, she said gamely, "Hi!"

"Hi yourself. You got something in your hand?"

"No, no."

"You got a splinter? You were digging at it when I opened the door."

"Oh, no. It's nothing."

"Let me see."

Arthur was "terrible big," as her pupils would say. Mary bet he weighed more than 250 pounds. His face was wide and craggy and sunburned, with deeply set blue eyes that looked like half-buried diamonds. His wife must be a terrific cook. Mam had often said those western women had a way with food. His hands reminded Mary of brown paws, thick fingers covered with fine hair. Hers looked white and freckled and dead. She was terrible ashamed of her sick-looking hands.

"Boy, you've got a doozy there. Hang on."

He stepped back, reached into his vest pocket, and produced a pair of tweezers. Taking her hand, he squeezed down hard with his thumb, jabbed at the protruding splinter, and pulled, then held it to the light.

"Largest splinter in Montana! A record!"

He laughed, a deep, easy sound that was unsettling. Mary had never heard anyone laugh quite so easily, as natural as breathing. Somehow she couldn't understand the emotion it evoked in her. She was just tired, overwrought.

"You ready?"

"I am. I thought I might have to plant my flag, being the only person to have set foot in Montana."

He laughed, deeper and more genuine than before, if such a thing was possible. "Ah. Hoo. A proper sense of humor. Boy, can we ever use you! Yeah, this drop-off point is a bit questionable. I wish they'd get rid of it and dump these city folks off at a more inhabited place. But this way. I came to get you with my buggy."

He carried her luggage as if it was filled with feathers, his long, swinging stride propelling him across the barrens, as Mary thought of the weed-choked clearing. By a grove of trees, a horse lifted his head, whinnied once, then again.

The buggy was unlike anything Mary had ever seen. It was wooden, but varnished instead of painted the usual black. It had no roof and only one seat, upholstered in a flamboyant shade of red with black buttons punched along the back. The wheels gleamed as if they were wet.

"Wow. Some ride," Mary observed.

"Nice, isn't it? I made it."

"Really? You built that buggy? Even the wheels?"

"Smart lady. No, of course not."

The only way to describe the sharing of the seat was that he had three-fourths of it and she had one-fourth. Mary felt very much like an afterthought, a pale, limp version of a human being.

"Good thing you're so tiny."

"Where do you put the children when you go away in this?"

Arthur's easy laugh rang out again. "Honey, I don't have children. To have some of those, you need a wife, and I don't have one of them, either."

Mary's face flamed until tears pricked her eyelids, making her blink fast to get rid of them. She looked steadily away from him to the left until she regained some sense of control over this runaway situation. If he'd stop laughing that laugh, she'd return to her normal self. Or taking the liberty of calling her "honey."

They rolled out onto a dirt road, bits of pale stone rattling around in the loose soil. Overhead, leafy trees mingled with beautifully shaped pines, the blue of the sky cut into bits and pieces by the dark green of the branches.

"Aren't you going to say anything about that?" he asked, suddenly.

"No. I just thought any school board member would naturally be married and have children attending the school."

"You're in Loma, Montana."

"Definitely not Lancaster County."

"You know, I've never been to that metropolis in my life."

"It's not a metropolis!"

"What is it then?"

His eyes crinkled again, almost burying the blue flash, and he let out another rolling sound of good humor.

Mary smiled and said, yes, it was sort of a city in some places, but not where she lived.

The dirt road dipped into hollows, then wound its way back out of them until they came to a vast, grassy, fenced-in area, with a bluish-purple mountain rising in the background, its highest peak covered in snow.

Involuntarily, Mary gasped.

Arthur pulled on the reins and stopped the buggy, allowing her to drink in the stunning landscape ahead of them. Mary leaned forward, then scooted to the edge of the red seat, clasped her hands, and formed an astonished O with her mouth. Finally, she sighed.

"Seriously." That was all she said.

Arthur watched Mary's pale face with the splattering of freckles. He watched the widening of her green eyes, took in the way the neckline of her blue-green dress was made so differently, the delicate collarbones beneath, and wondered.

Shyness was not one of his virtues, so he blurted out, "You don't seem to be encumbered with a husband either."

She acted like she didn't hear him at first, then turned to face him rather abruptly. "No."

"Care to tell me why?"

"Not really."

"Oh, come on."

"Let's just say my red hair and freckles scare men away."

Of course, that made him laugh again. Mary sat back against the cushions, crossed her arms over her waist, and stayed silent until the most adorable little schoolhouse she could imagine came into view. It was brown, built of graying lumber that had been stained. The roof was made of weathered-looking shingles. A stone chimney was laid meticulously along the outer back wall, and a small porch was built along the front. Six windows, also brown, had been installed on each side, allowing plenty of light and air for the children.

"Beaver Creek School."

"It is for sure the cutest thing ever," Mary said, slowly, her eyes taking in the rail fence, the ball field, all familiar and dear and yet so different. A few pines created an air of protection across the roof of the school, as if God had remembered the landscaping.

"I'm glad you like it."

"Where will I live?"

Arthur looked at Mary, all the creases around his eyes crinkled up, and he said offhandedly, "With me."

"But I can't. That would not be proper at all."

"Just kidding. Wanted to see what you'd say."

"Well."

"I'll show you."

Arthur tapped the reins on his horse's back, and they moved easily up the gradual slope away from the school.

They entered a small grove of trees where the dirt road turned left, winding along a small ravine. A fence began where the ravine ended, and Mary saw a herd of Black Angus cows, calves, and a massive bull, strolling along in the thick, lush grass. Off in the distance, a house was nestled below a large grove of towering pines.

It wasn't a house, Mary decided, as they approached, but more like a fancy shed. Her heart beat erratically now, her mouth turning as dry as Wheaties without milk.

Her spirits sank lower as they stopped in front of the primitive building. There was one window and one door. A narrow wooden porch with bowed timbers supported the sagging roof. Bits of wood and sodden newspaper were scattered along the steps, as if someone had started a fire a few years previously.

"This is it. You see now why I said you're going to live with me?"

Mary nodded. "It's not much, is it?"

"Sure isn't."

"I'll make it."

"If it's any help to you, my place is just across the pasture, but whatever you do, don't ever try crossing it. Eddie isn't one bit trustworthy."

"Eddie?"

"The bull."

"Oh."

"Come on. Get down. Make yourself at home. Obviously, there's no need to lock the door, so go on in."

Tentatively, Mary stepped down, then stood uncertainly as Arthur tied the horse.

"Go on in," he called.

She wasn't about to tell him she was afraid. She— Mary Stoltzfus—afraid. She had all the gumption, the nerve, the bravado anyone could possibly need, having honed her skills well with her earlier schoolchildren and their parents on more than one occasion. But she had never been over a thousand miles from home before with only a single other human being, an oversized teddy bear named Arthur Bontrager.

Taking a deep breath, she stepped up on the porch, wincing when the floorboards creaked and groaned. For the second time in one day, she turned a strange door knob both ways before shoving the ill-fitting door inside.

She blinked. "Well." She was pleasantly startled, which pulled up the corners of her mouth into a hesitant grin.

"It's cute! Oh, my word! It's clean! Well, look at this! Does the fireplace work? Where did someone come up with this kitchen island? This sink is so tiny! Does the refrigerator work? Oh, my! Look! The view! Aww!"

Clearly beside herself, Mary dashed from one large window to the next, opened spigots, swung doors back, then finally stopped, clasping both hands over her waist. "It's cute!" she said, suddenly self-conscious.

"The outside is pretty deceiving. I didn't get that far."

"You did this?"

"Yep, I did."

"Can I stay here tonight?"

"No."

"Why not?"

"There are mountain lions in these parts."

Mary faced him, her eyes wide.

Arthur chuckled. "Just kidding."

"Did the women clean this for me? Someone certainly did. There are clean towels in the bathroom."

"Yeah. Looks clean to me."

"I'm starved."

"Of course you are. I never thought that far. I don't know if the shelves are stocked or not. You better check. If there's nothing here, you could have supper with me."

A few basic staples were not supper, and Mary was beginning to feel extremely weak and lightheaded. She told Arthur she would accompany him to the house, but he'd have to bring her back for the night.

"You think?" he asked, his eyes almost closing when the creases folded themselves around them.

"I think."

The road to Arthur's house was hilly but pleasant, winding along low-lying ditches and gradually sloped groups of trees.

Meadowlarks and blue jays called across the pasture. He showed her where another Amish family, Kenny Yoders, lived. They had three boys in school, the troublemakers, everyone said.

"We'll see," Mary said, lifting her chin.

Arthur watched the way the evening sun set her hair on fire and thought she was probably right.

His house was built on a slope above the pasture, a huge log A-frame with mostly gleaming windows, decorated in the manner of most men—woolen blankets, elk and deer heads on the walls, rustic table and chairs, wide plank floors, scattered Indian rugs.

Mary was speechless. For the first time in her life, she felt truly inferior to another person, incapable of any pretense or swagger.

"The barn is below the house pretty far. That's one thing I'd change if I could. It was kind of short-sighted, placing the cow barn so far away." He spoke from behind the refrigerator door, banging containers. "How about some barbecue, coleslaw, pickles, and home fries?"

Mary nodded, walking slowly around the room. Suddenly she stopped. Lying flat on the surface of a small table was a photograph of a girl dressed in the typical western style of Amish clothes. It was unusual for anyone to have pictures lying around, so she touched it with the tips of her fingers, bit her lower lip, and looked at Arthur's broad back, turned to her as he let water run into the brown sink.

His girlfriend? Sister? Distant cousin? It would be rude to ask, so she didn't.

She kept a lively conversation going and accompanied him out to the front deck where they set their plates on a heavy iron patio table, pulled up comfortable chairs, and ate in companionable silence.

The barbecue was not the ground beef sloppy joes she was acquainted with, but slivers of slow-cooked beef with a sauce unlike anything she had ever tasted. The ice-cold coleslaw was a wonderful accompaniment, and the home fries, although not the same as fried potatoes at home, were absolutely delicious.

Mary leaned over her plate with the barbecue sauce going everywhere except where she wished it would, grabbed a second napkin, and swiped at her chin. Finally she sat back, caught Arthur's blue eyes, and said, "I don't know how to eat like a lady."

Arthur laughed, the same deep rumbling sound that came as easy and as natural as breathing. "I was just watching you tuck into your sandwich and wondered how in the world you manage to stay so thin?"

Mary shrugged. "My parents aren't heavy, and none of my siblings."

"How many do you have?"

"Ten."

"Wow. All thin?"

"Like rails."

"All red-haired?"

Mary shook her head, her mouth full. "No. Unfortunately. I'm a throwback. My Doddy Stoltzfus's side."

"What kind of a name is that? 'Stoltzfus'?"

"Not worse than 'Bontrager'!"

He laughed. The sun slid behind the distant purple mountain and the evening turned shadowy, but with a glow so ethereal, Mary was speechless.

Arthur said, "I don't think your red hair is unfortunate."

"Thank you. That's a compliment."

A shiver made Mary lean forward, grasping her forearms. "My, it cools off fast here in Montana."

Instantly, Arthur was on his feet. "Ruby left her sweater here last weekend. I'll get it for you."

Mary sat gazing at the scene before her, the majesty and wonder of it all. She had certainly never seen anything close to this. Unbidden, a lump appeared in her throat, again an emotion she did not understand.

A sweater was placed about her shoulders with a pat on her arm, and a resounding, "There you go."

"Thanks." Then, "I should go. Will you take me, please?"

When he didn't answer, she felt she had been too bold and said, "I can call a driver."

"You're definitely from Lancaster. A driver is likely ten miles away."

"Oh. Well, I'll walk."

"Stay awhile, Mary. You can sleep in the guest room. I'll go home with you in the morning."

Oh, well. He had a girlfriend, so no one would care.

She slept in a pair of flannel pajamas, made with yards and yards of fabric with moose antlers printed all over it, in a bed made of logs, with a down comforter and a mattress that came very close to bliss.

In Montana it was so dark and so quiet, Mary fell asleep with a smile on her face, eager to begin her new life. She'd try and make sure she was home for Christmas.

Chapter Three

The following day Mary examined every inch of her new domain and gave it a thorough cleaning with antibacterial Mr. Clean, hot water, and a rag. She polished windows and scrubbed the bathroom, then put her clothes away in the dresser with a large oval mirror.

She carefully set the few toiletries she'd brought in the cabinet above the bathroom sink, and she was finished.

The little house smelled clean but remained decidedly sterile. She looked forward to the delivery of everything she had shipped—her own quilts and comforters, towels, rugs, and some of the pictures and items she'd decorated with back home. She'd also sent clothes and shoes, but no furniture or dishes. She decided they were too expensive to ship and too unnecessary.

Her home was cozy, set under the pine and pin oak trees, just up the road from the school. It was dark brown, the vertical boards and batten stained to blend with the outdoors. Yes, the porch was small, the floorboards uneven, the steps rickety, and the posts bowed by the weather. But it was livable, if not opulent.

Now it was off to school. She tied the laces of her walking shoes, put on a clean black bib apron, and set off down the road, swinging her arms, breathing deeply, and drinking in the pure oxygen of this remote place where the hum of traffic, the smell of vehicle exhaust, paved roads, and smokestacks spewing black smoke, were unthinkable. What an assault that would be on these pure untouched leaves, dancing together in the strong mountain breeze, undisturbed by anything made by humans. It was all a wonder.

To her left, the sturdy board fence stood as a guard between her and the only threat she'd encountered so far, Eddie the bull.

Thick grasses waved and rippled in the wind, a never-ending sea of motion, rising and falling, dipping and swaying, responding to the air that swooped down from the mountains.

Mary grabbed her covering stings and tied them closely beneath her chin. Gravel crunched under the soles of her pounding footfalls as she increased her pace. She heard the children's chatter before she saw them. Three bicycles bore down on her, leaving little puffs of dust in their wake. She slowed, then came to a stop.

Three boys, like three peas in a pod, hatless, their thick blond hair windblown, their faces round, with eyes like blue almonds set in fringes of dark lashes, drew close.

They slowed, each one raising a hand, palm out, before increasing their speed, then lifted themselves off their seats to stand on the pedals of their bikes.

Without thinking, Mary called after them, "Hey!" Each bike braked to a halt, but not one of the boys turned to come back, so Mary walked after them.

"I would love to be introduced," she said.

"Yeah. We're Kenny Yoder's boys."

Aha.

"I'm the new teacher."

Silence clamped down on the boys, immobilizing them. They opened their mouths, closed them, and cast sidelong glances at each other before they checked Mary over from head to toe, taking in the red hair, the sneakers.

"How come your covering's weird?"

"I'm from Lancaster, Pennsylvania."

"See? I told you," one said loudly.

"Are you going to be my pupils?"

"Yeah."

"Good. I'm pleased to meet you. My name is Mary. Mary Stoltzfus."

She stepped closer and stuck out her hand, which each boy shook limply, but with a certain politeness.

"Your names?"

"I'm Junior."

"LaVonne."

"Matt."

"For Matthew?"

"Yeah."

"Good, good. Why don't you come with me? Show me around my new school?"

"Nope. We don't touch that place till we have to."

"Really? Why not?"

"We hate school."

"Oh, come on."

"We do." Earnestly, three heads nodded in unison, devoted to the cause of school-hating.

"Why?"

"It's boring."

"The teacher is mean as on old rooster."

"I doubt it."

"Huh! You weren't here!"

"Teachers are all the same. Every last one of those creatures is bent on making life miserable."

Mary laughed good-naturedly. "Well, you haven't met me yet, now have you?"

"Why would you be any different?"

"Hey, guys, give me a chance!"

The boys looked sideways at one another, raising their eyebrows in approval. She sounded pretty cool, actually. That David Mast would not have called them "guys."

Mary turned her head toward the schoolhouse. "You coming?"

"Nah. We'll wait till we have to go."

In unspoken agreement, they pedaled off. Mary stood and watched them go, a slight cloud passing over her features, but she turned and strode purposefully toward her new job. She had to climb over the fence, finding the gate securely locked against intruders. She wondered why Arthur had forgotten to provide a key for that first obstacle.

She unlocked the schoolhouse door, stepped into the one room, surveyed the interior with a sweeping glance, then put up a few blinds, unlocked windows, and raised them as well.

Hmm. Very interesting. It appeared as if the former teacher, David Mast, had not been able to spend all of fifteen minutes picking up paper plates and cups after the school picnic. Bits of Styrofoam were scattered all over the floor, with dried baked beans and blackened ketchup smeared over them.

Mary yelped when a small, brown mouse peeked from behind a desk leg. She dashed after the offensive animal, her foot slapping down a few inches behind the scurrying creature. When she made contact with it, she stomped down hard, lifted the lifeless rodent by its spindly tail, and flung it out the door. She killed three more that afternoon, whacking the disgusting mice with the heavy straw broom, and disposing of them as efficiently as the first one.

She made a thorough search of the baseboard, looking for any possible mouse entrances, found none, and reasoned that they must have coexisted with David Mast and his scholars. Gross. Well, consider your happy homes invaded. I do not live with mice.

She swept the wide plank floors, burned the garbage, and took stock of all the supplies, checking carefully the list she had made for herself, muttering under her breath as she did so.

The schoolroom looked a lot like the one back home except for the wooden flooring. The used metal desk was beige, like hers, the wooden seats fastened to the floor the way she was used to. The walls were white with oak wainscoting along the lower half. A round clock with large numbers hung on the west wall. There was the usual gray file cabinet, a large, cast iron woodstove, a cloakroom with hooks, shelves for lunchboxes, and a stand with a Rubbermaid dishpan for hot water and soap to wash hands before lunch.

Yes, indeed. It was all different, yet familiar. She found the parents' names and their telephone numbers. She'd call and leave messages with each one, telling them she had decided to have the school cleaning the following Tuesday.

She was surprised to find the classroom suddenly bathed in the evening glow that meant the sun was already low, and setting quickly. Hurriedly, she lowered the windows, pulled the blinds, locked the door, and let herself out, surprised to find the shadows already lengthened and deepening fast.

She scrambled over the fence, turned her head both ways twice out of habit, before realizing there was no traffic to look out for, and scuttled sheepishly up the road. She hoped no one had seen her. No one would have, since there wasn't a single soul anywhere.

A deep sense of melancholy enveloped her, silencing the song in her mind, the energy with which she'd ticked off one job after another all afternoon. She felt weary and very, very alone.

She would come home to an empty house. She could not run across the porch to her parents to share her day with them. Homesickness clenched her stomach, stopping her breathing. Her steps slowed, she bent her head, and for only an instant, nothing made sense.

Why was she here, propped up by all this false bravado? If she would have followed her instincts, she would have told those unkind boys to go home and stay there and not to bother coming to school at all with their stinking attitudes.

She had nothing to eat and no idea where there was a grocery store. Should she call Arthur? Why not?

She forgot. She had no telephone. If she did, she hadn't been able to find it. When she arrived at the small brown house, she searched along the back for any kind of shed or addition that could house a telephone, but there was none.

Well, she'd have to make do. Searching the cupboards, she found oatmeal, then carried the container to the doorway to check for bugs. Sure enough, the flakes of oatmeal were moving around as if they had a life of their own.

She found salt, pepper, seasonings, flour, and a bit of sugar in a bag that was as hard as a rock. She could soak the hardened sugar with warm water and sip it like a hummingbird. Not very nutritious. Or appealing.

Well, she had to eat. She could walk to Kenny Yoder's, but if the parents were anything like their boys, she'd probably be chased off the property by a Rottweiler or a pit bull.

She'd go to Arthur. If she didn't think of him as eligible, she wouldn't become tongue-tied and flustered. He was definitely not eligible.

Oh, she could act as unconcerned, as uncaring about her singledom as she wanted, but it was still there. She had never been chosen. She had never been asked. Never. At first, she had minded. She had hurt worse than anyone could ever tell. Rejection filled the sails that were her pride, and she moved through life with that wind propelling her, keeping her head high, a smile on her face.

Eventually she stopped caring, then stopped "running around," that time of *rumspringa* when she went with the youth. She was that young, thin-as-a-rail, red-haired girl who attended all her friends' weddings, one by one, as the young men labeled "hopefuls" in her mind turned to someone else.

She'd blamed her looks, hating her red hair. She despised her freckles, her pale skin, her too-thin body, her skinny ankles with the size nine shoes slapping like flippers on the ground as she walked. She was awkward, that was what it was, she decided. Ugly and ungainly. But not stupid or dumb.

School had been a whiz for her. She read like a starving person. Ravenously. She devoured words, mulled them around in her brain like a fine wine—or the way she imagined fancy people tasted wine.

When the school board asked her to teach, she said yes, then threw herself into her new role whole-heartedly. The children filled her heart, her thin, empty arms. She held her first-graders on her lap, shared her potato chips with them, listened to their sweet, lisping voices, and fell in love over and over again.

School-teaching became a haven, a safe, warm place where she felt no need for pretense. Gradually, the lack of romance in her life receded, stuffed in a drawer. Mary inserted the key, turned it, and threw it away. Clearly God wanted her to be single. He didn't plan for her to marry and have children. She was a leftover blessing, a real gift to the Amish community. *An goota* teacher.

In Lancaster, her guest bedroom was filled with ceramics with thoughtful-teacher slogans all over them. She had boxes of wooden plaques with beautiful verses. Towels, sheets, framed artwork, pieces of furniture, Princess House items, Pampered Chef cookware, Tupperware containers from parties held in her honor—material things, but only the finest—piled around her until she felt buried in them. They were meant to show appreciation and thanks. Thank you. Thank you. Thank you.

But never once had a young man asked for her hand.

With that thought hovering over her, she showered and then combed her wet hair carefully, wishing it would stay that deep auburn color after it dried. She dressed in a clean, although slightly wrinkled, dress that was a deep shade of brown, tied her black apron over it, put on her clean covering, and let herself out the door.

Twilight had settled across the countryside, throwing the mountains into a deep shade of velvet. The wind had finally stilled except for a few rustling leaves.

Almost she lost her nerve. It made her angry, this shrinking inside herself when she felt even remotely attracted to someone. She thought she'd successfully subdued any emotion that pertained to young men, or, since she was older, to any men.

She could not imagine, if someone as, well, as interesting as Arthur Bontrager would. . . . Well, he wouldn't. Mary, he wouldn't. A mental picture suddenly dangled in front of her eyes. Okay, God, I know. Thank you for reminding me.

Just when she thought she'd successfully squelched all emotion or attraction to him, she thought of the tanned creases around his eyes, the sound of his laugh. Oh, mercy. Mary, stop.

She hurried on up the winding, wooded slope to his house, the board fence on her right, the shadows deepening steadily. A cow's lowing, the distant yipping of a dog, an answering bellow.

A bellow? She stopped, her eyes searching the dim light of the pasture. She could barely discern the shape of the black cows. She shivered when the sound came again. More like a roar. Eddie was mad.

The last hundred yards her feet flew across the lane. She was panting, her chest heaving, when she pounded on the door. Thank goodness, there was a yellow light shining from the living room.

Arthur let her in, surprised at her agitation, listening carefully when she described the sound.

"Eddie's just letting everyone know who's boss," he said, then laughed. His eyes crinkled, and he asked her to sit down.

"I will. I'll fall over of starvation if I don't."

Arthur became clearly upset. He had never thought of her lack of groceries. He apologized profusely, over and over, then heated a large serving of ham and potato chowder and brought saltines, sour pickles, cold beef, sliced tomatoes, sliced onions, butter, mustard, and mayonnaise. He told her when he watched her eat the barbecue he knew that she was a real lover of sandwiches.

She bent her head and slurped her chowder and spoke with her mouth full. She used three napkins, drank two glasses of tea, and watched his blue eyes appear and disappear when he laughed or when he became serious. She ate a large wedge of apple pie, bursting with brown sugar, butter, and cinnamon, and topped with vanilla ice cream and caramel syrup.

He put extra groceries in a box for her, then promised to accompany her to the local Amish bulk food store in the morning.

"You can't walk home alone. I'll put this box on the express wagon and go with you."

"I'll manage."

"What about Eddie?"

"I'll be all right."

"No. You're not going home alone. I let you starve, now I won't let you be in danger. You could stay with me."

"Oh, no. I can't."

"Why not?"

"Well," Mary shrugged her shoulders helplessly. She wanted to say, what about her, the girl in the photograph? I know I'm a homely old maid, but I have never been so desperate that I would do anything to hurt someone else.

"Well, what? Just stay. I want you to hear the wolves."

"What wolves?" The words came sharply. Mary was frightened.

"The wolves."

"I hadn't realized there were wolves."

"Oh, there are."

He made coffee, laced it liberally with cream, sugar, and a shot of hazelnut flavoring, then provided his girlfriend's sweater. They sat on the great, rustic log chairs on the patio under the vast, velvet sky dotted with twinkling white stars.

They talked about his work building log furniture, the cows, the state of Montana. They wandered into conversation about the Amish who choose to live away from the curious eyes of tourists, about growing communities that are troubled by unfortunate events caused by greed or jealousy or "other maladies of human nature," as Mary pointed out. She was rewarded by a great, rolling laugh.

They fell silent. Mary sat in awe of the night, the way the stars seemed to lower themselves, blink, then blink again, before resuming their normal place. She was just opening her mouth and catching her breath when she heard the first distant sound. At first she thought it was the neighbor's dog. Arthur held up a hand, then set down his mug and motioned for her to come.

"Listen closely."

From far away across the treetops and the darkened pasture, the sound began, low at first, then building to a long, undulating howl, a wail of loneliness and sorrow, a sound of longing, a primitive, beautiful cry that was almost spiritual. God wanted them to know that He had made this night, the vast, dark sky, the blinking stars, the howling of these, his creatures.

Unbidden, a sob tore from Mary's throat. Terrified of her own weakness, she covered her face with both hands and turned away, determined to hide the fact that the wolves' howling had stirred her soul. When the sound came again, she remained rigid, ashamed of her emotion, desperately blinking back the unwelcome tears.

She felt, rather than saw, Arthur's presence as he came close. She heard his voice.

"It's always interesting to me, to see a person's response when they hear the wolves for the first time."

Even if she had wanted to, she couldn't have answered, so she stayed as she was, head bent, her hands covering her face.

"I have never heard anyone cry." Gently, his big hands held her shoulders. Slowly, he turned her around until she faced him. Miserably, she let her hands fall away where they hung awkwardly at her sides beside her size nine feet.

Mary swallowed, then whispered, "It's the most beautiful sound I've ever heard."

When he drew her against his wide, wide chest and his great arms went around her, she laid her head against the flannel of his shirt, closed her eyes, and wept. He laid his cheek on the top of her head, the way he would comfort a small child, which made Mary cry more.

Again the wolves howled, sending chills up Mary's spine. She stepped back, straining to hear, then smiled up at Arthur through her tears.

"The most overused word in the English vocabulary and it's all I can think of—awesome. Absolutely awesome." Self-conscious now, and much too close to Arthur, she tried to step out of the circle of his arms. This was completely unseemly. She was so thoroughly ashamed.

For a moment, she thought he would release her, but he only gathered her into a long, comforting embrace. She heard him sigh, and then suddenly, she stood chillingly alone.

"Mary. Mary."

That was all he said. They walked home side by side, Arthur pulling the express wagon with the box of groceries. They walked in silence, carrying the magic of the night with them.

He promised to pick her up at nine o'clock in the morning with the team, then wished her a good night and left, the wagon bumping behind him.

Mary lay sleepless far into the night. She had never been held in an embrace by a man. She must never go to his house again. She knew deep down she could not approach him about the girl in the photograph. As long as she didn't know for sure, she could remain unaware. She would have to extricate herself before Arthur became someone she could not live without.

Chapter Four

THE AIR WAS ALREADY TINGED WITH WHISPERS OF fall by the last week in August when the bell on top of the schoolhouse rang on the first day of school. Mary stood inside yanking the rope, letting the bell peal its message across the valley, letting it roll on and on till it bumped against the mountains, unsettled the snow on top, perhaps starting an avalanche. Who knew?

She was in her element. She felt strong, in control, and capable. She had met the schoolchildren and their parents the week before and was pleasantly surprised to find them friendly, eager to be introduced, and willing to help. She was an expert at parent evaluation. Mrs. Kenny Yoder was the only rotten apple in the bunch, she could plainly tell. And even she might not be too difficult.

She had been completely enamored of the little girls with their stiff white coverings propped on their heads like neat little cups. Their hair was done so differently than Lancaster girls', whose hair was wet down flatly against their heads, the sides rolled in tightly, and the buns on the backs of their heads just as severe. These little girls' hair was combed naturally up toward the middle of their heads. And here their pinafore-type aprons were the same color as their dresses.

They were happy, well cared for, secure, and eager to learn, as far as Mary could tell.

The pealing of the bell brought the twenty-one pupils crashing through the door and sliding into their desks, after they each found their name tags stuck onto the upper right-hand corner with Scotch tape.

They watched Mary openly, unabashedly. This new teacher dressed so differently, and she was, indeed, very interesting.

The singing class was the first sign of the work ahead. The two eighth-grade boys sagged against the blackboard, their hands stuffed into their denim trousers, each refusing to hold a songbook with a girl.

Mary took notice, clasped her songbook to her chest, and said clearly, "Allen and Danny, you may go back to your seats."

They looked perplexed.

"You obviously do not enjoy singing, so you may sit down."

Snickering, they walked back to their seats. The remainder of the class watched Mary, unsure of how to proceed.

"All right. We'll start with the oldest person, and each morning three of you may choose the song you would like to sing. Alma?"

The only girl in eighth grade raised her hand. "That's not how we did it last year."

"That's all right. This year, we'll do it this way."

Mary made sure her smile reached each one. Alma chose number 248, and the room was filled with quiet and discordant strains of "Will the Circle be Unbroken?".

Halfway through the song, Mary held up a hand. Half of them were not singing, and she asked why. Mary encouraged them to open their mouths and put their hearts into the music. Then she launched into a solo, a rousing rendition of "John Brown Had a Little Indian."

Grins behind songbooks turned to titters of amusement, and then to wide smiles as Mary continued to sing at the top of her voice.

"By Christmas, we'll really bring the house down!" she chortled.

After that, Mary had the pupils' complete attention. She was experienced and knew what boosted morale, understanding that most children who "hated" school only needed to find fresh interest. Each day she set about pursuing her goal of having a classroom filled with eager children, anxious to please, happy to come to school. By the time the frost lay heavily in the hollows, the Montana community was buzzing with praise for the red-haired teacher from Lancaster. They said they'd never seen anything like it. Harley Miller's children counted the hours till they could go to school. And did you see her artwork?

Mary attended church services for the first time at Elmer Helmuth's place, transported in the back of Kenny Yoder's spring wagon. She felt like an owl in a flock of pigeons, the way she knew she would, but she was a comfortable owl, quite secure in her owlness. She knew the parents thought highly of her, signaled by the handclasps and the fawning, the praise heaped on her shoulders.

Yes, she was indeed capable, turning the school into a lean, efficient learning machine. So she moved among these western people dressed according to a different *ordnung,* confident, smiling, pouring coffee at the dinner table. She went home with Marvin Troyers and had a wonderful evening playing Scrabble, which she won, of course. Every game, too.

Only at night alone in the little house did she let the loneliness of her heart unravel. She no longer went to Arthur's house. She told him coolly after the night the wolves howled that she could easily make it on her own, that she'd appreciated his help, but it wasn't proper to be spending all this time together.

"I've overstepped my boundaries, haven't I?" he'd said, his creases all gone, his eyes large and blue and serious.

"Well, no. Not really. I just need to stay in my place."

"Which is?"

"Alone."

He'd raised his eyebrows at that and left her alone. Every weekend his house stayed dark, until sometime late Sunday evening, he'd return.

She even went about, in her cunning way, deriving information about Arthur's weekend meanderings, finding out which other Amish communities were nearby, but never directly asking about his girlfriend's existence. She was extremely efficient at teaching school, and she told herself that she would become as efficient at removing Arthur Bontrager from her head, where he stuck like an unwanted virus. She was always in control, so she would be able to take care of this disorder, this letting down of the iron guard around her heart.

It was only at night when she relived the magic of being held in his arms, cradling the memory, nurturing it, and telling herself that if it was all she ever had, as far as a bit of romance in her life, it would suffice. No, she had never been asked, never been chosen, but she had been held against Arthur's great chest and heard the heavy thudding of his heart. That was something, wasn't it?

When the leaves began to change their colors from many shades of green to golden yellows, reds, and oranges, wood fires were lit in stoves all over the community. Smoke rose from well-built chimneys as split wood was crammed into stoves. Warmth spread through houses, making them cozy places where adults gathered next to woodstoves, their spirits lifting.

Mary hadn't thought about her source of heat. She flipped the knob on the gas stove, turned the oven on, and let its heat warm the little house quite efficiently. She'd never given the lean-to in the back of the house much thought. She knew it was filled with split wood, but never really thought about it being her source of heat. She was too busy being capable.

So when the leaves shivered and fell to the ground, when the air turned wet and cold with the chance of snow falling, Mary woke up one Saturday morning, late, her nose like an icicle. Her legs hurt, her back was stiff, and she was, quite simply, freezing.

Well, she could lie here and be miserable, or she could get up, get dressed, and start a fire. Wistfully, she thought of home where the thermostat on the wall would turn on the propane gas heater and fill the house with quiet, efficient heat. She wanted to go shopping today and then go out for lunch with Sarah Ann, her friend.

She wanted to eat at Applebee's, a place where they served different food than she ate at home, with inappropriate music, for her, perhaps, but where anything you ordered was so good. She missed the traffic, the bustle of the fall harvest, the weddings.

Groaning, she rolled out of bed, tiptoed swiftly to the gas range, and turned the oven on. Seriously, that was like lighting a candle in an igloo, but every little bit helped, she supposed. She opened the door a crack, yelped, banged it shut, and said, "Shoo!" It was very earnestly, quite cold. Decidedly, grievously cold out there.

Shivering, she dressed in the heaviest weight dress she owned, threw a sweater on, followed by her black lightweight windbreaker, buttoning it all the way down. She put a white scarf on her head, two pairs of woolen socks on her feet, and her leather snow boots on top of them. Pulling on a heavy pair of gloves, she went to the lean-to for wood, then carried a few small sticks to the house, shivering, and complaining under her breath. She had never started a wood fire.

Slowly she opened the door of the cast iron stove and peered inside. Hmm. It was very dark in there.

Going to the pantry, she found her flashlight hanging from a peg, clicked it on, and directed its beam into the stove. Looked like lots of ashes. She needed a poker. Isn't that what you called those cast iron things?

Searching the wall behind the stove, she found a short, heavy cast iron thing that had a hook on the end. Some people just had no common sense. Couldn't they see a poker needed to be a lot longer? She grasped the little thingy, as she dubbed it, and scraped away inside the stove, hurting the inside of her arm as she moved it back and forth across the rough edges.

"Ow!" She sat back on her haunches and checked the sleeve of her windbreaker, horrified to see the holes that she had just worn through it. There had to be a better way.

Going to the pantry again, she lifted the broom down from its hook, then inserted the handle into the woodstove and vigorously scraped it back and forth. That was better. When she was satisfied that most of the ashes had been pushed down through the grates, she opened the bottom door and yanked at the ash pan, then hollered as a cloud of ashes tumbled out over the pan, rolled across the clean floor, and drifted up into her face.

"Whew!" Taking the corner of her apron she waved it madly, which only dislodged more of the wood ashes, sending them flying in every direction.

Frustrated, she grabbed the pan, lurched through the door, down the steps and across the yard, where she flung the offending ashes into the wind the wrong way. They all wafted neatly over her entire body, leaving her choking and coughing, her mouth and eyes turning black where the ashes met with moisture.

Hateful old woodstoves. Lifting her black apron, she began flopping it about, trying to rid herself of all the offending ashes.

She slammed the cottage door behind her, inserted the ash pan, and stood, eyeing the door of the woodstove. Now what? Newspaper. Kindling. She had no axe. Or hatchet. Well, maybe the smallest pieces would catch fire.

Her hands stiff with the cold, her stomach rumbling, she crumpled the paper, then carefully laid the smallest stick of wood on top, held a Bic lighter to it, and was rewarded by greedy yellow flames devouring the paper.

Well, that was odd. The smoke was supposed to go up the chimney. Not out of this door. She coughed. A sneeze racked her body. Now what?

She removed the stick of wood, then crumpled more paper, arranged it carefully again, and lit the paper. More black smoke poured into her face the second time.

Stamping her foot, Mary yelled, "You dumb, ignorant stove!"

For a third time, she tried the same procedure—with the very same result. Mary slammed the stove door as hard as she could, then kicked the small door at the bottom. Pain shot through her big toe, and she sank to the brown sofa, holding the painful toe in both hands, thinking she might pass out flat on the floor.

She was licked. Beaten. She'd walk to Kenny Yoder's and ask for their help. The boys could come back with her.

But first, she had to eat. Flopping the skillet on top of the stove, she flipped the burner on, then placed both hands above it, letting the heat move through the palms of her hands. Blessed, wonderful warmth.

She fried two eggs, grilled two slices of bread, slurped down some lukewarm coffee, and set out for Kenny Yoder's, her toe throbbing painfully.

Swinging her arms while moving along at a frantic pace, she caught a movement out of the corner of her eye. A flash of brown. Mary stopped, hoping to catch sight of a deer. Or perhaps one of those elusive coyotes that was so afraid of humans. Instead, she was faced squarely by two of the largest dogs she had ever seen. Their heads were round and square at the same time, wide between their eyes, one more black than brown. Flat, wicked eyes, like serpents', looked back at her. Their huge slavering mouths, with white teeth exposed, grinned at her as they panted.

Mary backed away. Somewhere she had read not to make eye contact. Don't run. Don't panic.

She turned, walking back the way she had come, her back rigid with fear. She willed herself to keep looking ahead and not to look back.

She heard them. She heard their feet. Then she heard their breathing. Rasping breaths, coming fast.

Yet she kept walking. She wanted to break into a run, just run and run, but she knew it was futile. She would never be able to outrun these powerful creatures.

Dear God. Help. Help me. She was sobbing now.

Closer. The breathing was much closer.

Mary ran. The only instinct she could obey was to run. The heavy socks and snow boots held her back, but she kept lunging forward, willing herself more speed. Past the school. She was almost home. Her breath tore at her throat. Her chest felt as if it was on fire. She looked back.

Two more steps, and she was flung to the ground by the force of the black dog driving his body into her shoulder. She screamed and screamed as jaws attached themselves to the calf of her leg. She cowered on all fours, her head bent, and kept screaming. The grip on her boot released. Turning, she kicked out with both legs as the horrible beasts circled her.

Screaming again, she rolled, got to her feet, and turned to run as the dogs' jaws clamped around her leg again. She was thrown to the ground, bouncing with the impact. The back of her head was flung hard against the frozen soil, and she thought, "This is how I'll die."

Still she screamed, hoping someone, anyone, would hear.

When the second dog's jaws gripped her forearm, its teeth tearing away at her sweater and windbreaker, then sinking into the soft flesh, she stopped screaming. Whimpering and crying, she begged the dogs to go away.

The next hit was directly in her face, the jaws snapping on her white headscarf as she twisted away. She covered her head with both hands and rolled onto her stomach as the dog's jaws clamped onto her leg yet again. The leather snow boot took most of the impact, saving her leg. She kicked at the solid, hairy body, then swiped at the lust in the greedy black eyes with her gloved hands.

She let out scream after scream until her voice was silenced by the impact of the dog's jaws on her cheekbone, tearing away at her face. She twisted away as blood filled her vision, turning the beautiful Montana landscape to red.

She didn't hear the shot. She felt the dog go slack, the one in her red vision, the one attached to her shoulder. He let his jaws relax, and Mary rolled away. As she rolled twice, she heard the sharp crack of a gunshot. The dog yelped, his flat eyes registered shock, and he rolled away, limp.

Mary lay curled in a tight position as wave after wave of searing pain tore through her body. She knew she was losing blood by the lightheaded, nauseous feeling that swept through her. She had to get home. Placing both hands on the ground, she steadied herself, willed herself to sit upright. She would not lose consciousness. Not now. She had to get home.

One knee was on the ground. There. She could get to her feet. With a gigantic effort, she got up on all fours. She began crying, failure seeping into her knowing. That was where Arthur Bontrager found her, saying over and over, "I can't, I can't."

Blood covered her face and soaked into her thick, red hair. Her boot was half chewed off; her coat hung in tatters. Arthur lost no time. He picked her up like an injured rag doll, strode off down the road, and laid her on the floor of her house. He went to the wood-shed where they'd installed the telephone and called the nearest neighbor, then ran to apply torn strips of cloth above her wounds. He placed a towel under her head and knew there was nothing else he could do. Mary was conscious, her eyes wide.

Wiping the blood away as best he could, Arthur asked if she was all right until they got to a doctor.

"I'll be fine," she whispered. She gritted her teeth and closed her eyes as Arthur and his helper propped her up in the middle, between them, in the old pickup truck. Not once did she cry out as the truck barreled across the ruts and potholes in the rural, gravel road.

She spoke clearly to the doctor, giving him the needed information herself, and assured Arthur that there was no need to take her to a hospital.

He waited outside, pacing the floor, as the doctor sutured the wounds. He did a good job on her eyelid, placing tiny stitches to hold it together. He repaired the hole in her cheek with nine neat little stitches. Like quilting, he told her. She smiled a very small smile. She told the doctor she supposed she was one fortunate person.

After two hours of repair work, the doctor called "her husband" back into the treatment room, which put a permanent amount of creases around Arthur's eyes for quite some time.

Arthur would not give up. It was the only sensible thing to do. She was not staying alone. She would stay with him. She stopped protesting when the truck seemed to tilt sideways and spin around in the opposite direction. She reasoned to herself, made excuses, then nodded in agreement.

Arthur paid the driver, then carried her into the house and sat her on the recliner, while he hurried from room to room, gathering sheets and pillows, blankets, a small table, a pitcher of ice water, pain pills, and a box of Kleenex.

With the room spinning wildly, her head fell back as he carried her to the wide, deep sofa. He thought she'd fainted until her eyelids fluttered and she tried to thank him, but couldn't.

When she fell asleep, he sat beside her watching every twitch of pain, every rise and fall of her chest, and wondered again at the way her collarbones rose from the neckline of her dress. Somehow, they were the only vulnerable thing about her.

Chapter Five

BACK IN HER OWN HOUSE, WITH THE CHIMNEY properly cleaned, a wood fire crackled cozily. Mary's wounds healed as the weather turned increasingly colder. The snow that had waited behind protective layers of clouds tumbled down in fine, icy bits, turning the countryside into a frigid world of pure white.

Tomorrow she would go back to school. The concerned parents had taken turns keeping the school going for a few weeks, but Mary anticipated—no, *expected*—nothing short of pure chaos. Her record book would be inaccurate, if it had been kept at all. She had plenty of experience where substitutes were concerned; she would leave the house in the morning prepared for bedlam.

And now Arthur wanted her to get a dog. That was quite unnecessary, thank you very much. She had no use for those creatures, especially big ones. If they had pet day at school, she admired the yipping little nuisances from a distance, kept up false praises for the big, drooling ones, but could never feel any affection for man's best friend. They smelled, for one thing. They barked and barked, turned somersaults, and leaped senselessly in the air for no apparent reason other than their own stupidity. They shed fine hair over floors and chairs and sofas.

She had plenty of single friends in Lancaster who owned little white or black or brown dogs that leaped up into her lap, wrongly assuming they were welcome. So she grinned half-heartedly, scratched their ears once, then unobtrusively wiped her fingers on a handkerchief once the small dog had the good sense to jump off her lap.

The thing was, it was rude to push precious Daisy or Belle or Oscar off her lap. She had to restrain herself quite often, however, when every fiber of her being wanted to send the dog none too gently off her lap.

So, no, she did not want a dog or need one.

Arthur had instructed her in the ways of wood fires. She was a fast learner, quite efficiently raking down the coals with the long-handled poker, (the short one with the hook on the end was for shaking the grates) adding heavy split logs, closing the damper when she was away, and adjusting the thermostat. She felt capable now, a seasoned woodstove handler.

Marching smartly down the road, swinging her lunchbox and book satchel, breathing in the snappy, cold air, the soles of her boots crunching in the frozen snow, Mary felt on top of the world once again. Sutures removed, vitamin E capsules sent for from the store called Nature's Warehouse, B&W salve applied—it was all taken care of.

What was that? Wildly, she turned her head to the left, then to the right. Twigs snapped. Stopping, her breath coming in ragged puffs, Mary searched the trees and brush by the roadside. There it was. Oh. Oh, my goodness. A flash of brown. Unable to believe that God would ever allow more vicious dogs to attack, she remained standing, rooted to the snowy ground, as more twigs snapped.

The two deer that emerged from the undergrowth turned their heads, their wide, almond-shaped ears held erect, as they watched a heavily dressed schoolteacher hustle clumsily down the road, swinging her satchels as if they could help propel her faster.

Mary's hand shook as she tried inserting the key into the lock. She took a few deep breaths to steady herself before attempting it the second time.

As she had feared, the schoolroom was a mess. Crumpled papers were strewn haphazardly across the floor, gray stains showed where juice or soup had spilled, wrinkled aluminum foil covered leftover food forgotten on the stove, sending out a mildly burnt odor.

Her usual precise stack of corrected workbooks were thrown onto the table in the middle aisle with a half-done puzzle beside them. Markers and broken crayons were everywhere.

Mary surveyed the room, deciding that a father had likely taught on Friday. She pushed up her sleeves and set to work. She swept the puzzle into the box propped up beside it and snapped the lid down over it, then picked up crayons, straightened the workbooks, grabbed a broom, and winced at the amount of dust that puffed up with every draw.

The schoolroom was halfway in order when the pupils began to arrive. Mary greeted them all with genuine gladness, showed them her scars, then pulled up a chair to the fire and gathered the children around her for a long and detailed discussion about the stray dog attack.

They skipped arithmetic that morning, which was, indeed, the most wonderful thing any teacher could think of. They touched Mary's scars, some of them shyly, others yelping when they felt the hard ridge where the sutures had held the cut in place.

The upper-grade boys said it was necessary for her to own a dog.

Mary shook her head. "I don't like dogs."

"Why not? I don't know anyone that doesn't like dogs," Kenny Yoder's Matt said, frustrated.

"What could one dog have done to save me?" Mary asked.

"Everything!" the boys shouted, clapping their hands, then launched into a long and detailed account of Ranger, the German Shepherd's brave stand-off with a catamount.

"Whatever that is," Mary murmured.

"A lion."

"Not an African, maned lion."

"No, a mountain lion. Cougar. Panther. A big cat."

Mary laughed heartily. "I get it."

They finished their talk with plans for Christmas, which was coming fast. Mary told them they would need to begin practicing directly after Thanksgiving for the program.

Howls of protest went up. Mary could not believe what she was hearing. "Why? Don't you want a Christmas play?"

"No, no, no!" They shook their heads back and forth, denying her any anticipation of the usual Christmas celebration.

Wisely, Mary decided to drop it. She tapped the small bell on her desk, restored order, resumed classes, and marched into her usual efficient routine. She was glad of it, too.

Who could have known, she thought? How could she possibly have foreseen that her biggest challenge to overcome was the mere walk to and from school? She was absolutely petrified, especially now when at five o'clock, long eerie shadows fell across the road.

Sheepishly, making sure no one saw her, she went to the school's woodshed and rummaged around in the blue Rubbermaid garbage can until she found a good-sized baseball bat. She picked a wooden one that went unnoticed, since the children always chose the aluminum ones with popular slogans inscribed on them.

Mary lifted it and swung it in a circle. Aha. This would do nicely. Baseball bats were efficient as far as bloodthirsty dogs were concerned, and they didn't smell and bark raucously at any small rodent or bee. Once at a picnic down at Pequea Park, Sarah Fisher's Pekingese had eaten a bee, then threw up so horribly, Mary thought she would have to stand by as the pathetic little creature met his demise.

Mary started off, her book satchel slung over her shoulder, the bat gripped in the same hand as her lunchbox. She was all set. She kept her eyes on the road and tried hard to ignore the vast shadows, the thin branches of the undergrowth, the great, deep green, pine branches drooping with the added burden of snow.

She would not look. She would keep steadfastly on course. The wind kicked up, moving the pine branches. Whump!

Mary screamed hoarsely, then dropped her satchel, whirled around, her feet apart, her back lowered, gripping the bat, the panic propelling the breath from her mouth. What was that?

Shamefaced, she lowered the bat, took up her satchel, and continued on her way. She couldn't be too aware, now could she?

With her breath coming in short puffs, she clattered up onto her porch, propped the bat against the wall, fumbled for the silver band that held her key, and opened the door, glancing back at the darkening path that led from the road to her door.

There were still a few red coals lying on the grate, which meant she'd need a few small sticks of wood. Once they burned well, she could add larger pieces. Slapping her hands together, she rid herself of the sawdust and watched the dry bark flame up, then closed the door with a pleasing, experienced bang.

She flicked the blue Bic lighter beneath the two white Coleman mantles, turned the knob, and was rewarded by a burning white light, sufficiently chasing away the deepening gloom in the corners. For an instant, she longed for the ease of her gas heat in Lancaster, but soon let it pass, deciding there was nothing to be gained by pitying oneself, or wishing for something you couldn't have.

Oh, what was she hungry for? Nothing really. She had too many papers to correct. She put the tea kettle on the gas burner, threw a mint tea bag in her favorite mug, spread out the papers and answer book, grabbed the red Bic pen, and began.

The low moaning of the wind turned into a more urgent sound. The window by the table rattled. Mary shivered as a draft of cold air snaked across the floor. Getting up, she peeled off her black nylons, stuck her feet into a pair of old fleece socks, then pushed them into her deerskin slippers.

Very feminine, she thought, smiling to herself. But who cared? There was no one to see, no one to impress with her choice of footwear. She glanced wryly at her slippers. Perhaps they were men's slippers. They looked like it. She had always disliked her feet. They wouldn't be quite so out of proportion if she was heavier, but as it was, being so thin, her feet were big boats housed in men's slippers. She really hated them.

The tea kettle whistled, and she poured boiling water over the tea bag, added sugar, and stirred.

The sound of a diesel engine caught her attention. Quickly, she went to the door, peering out through the beige, homespun fabric. There stood an English man with a gigantic dog that looked the same at both ends. Mary squinted her eyes, looking for the difference between the dog's head and its tail.

Well, the man looked nice. When he knocked, she opened the door immediately, stepped aside, and asked him in. She stepped back much further when the man put a hand on the dog's collar and brought him along inside, too, just as if it was human.

Already, Mary felt the presence of dog hair. It would waft through the air, she'd breathe it in through her nostrils, and it would clog the air passage in her throat.

The man touched the brim of his camouflage cap. "Evening, ma'am."

"Good evening."

"Hey, Art told me you needed a dog."

"Oh, he did?"

"Yeah, I raise these 'uns.'"

Mary crossed her arms, raising her eyebrows. "Really?"

"Yeah, they're good dogs. Mighty expensive, but if you lay out the money, you know you'll have complete protection from anyone who mistreats you, any wild animal, anything. They're extremely loyal. Completely fearless. They don't smell, slobber, or shed. They're smart as a tack. They're a real highfalutin' dog. I'll let you have a six-month-old one for two thousand."

Mary eyed the man levelly, then looked at the dog, which was so black it could melt into the night and you'd never know it. The animal was huge, with hair all over its eyes. She didn't believe for one minute he didn't smell, slobber, or shed. What a salesman!

"That's all right," Mary said quickly. "I can't really afford him. I'm not sure I need a dog just yet."

The dog lifted its head. Its eyes were as black as its hair. No wonder she couldn't tell which end was which.

"He'll get bigger yet. This one's gonna be big."

"I'm sure."

"Oh, forgot to innerduce myself."

Mary took the proffered hand, her shoulders snapping forward when he shook it with the force of a sledge hammer. She wondered if her thumb would ever be the same.

"Bob Lewis Armstrong."

"I'm Mary."

"Yes, yes. Art said you were the new teacher. Said dogs got you. Mark my words, there's always them strays. Worse 'n wolves. Keeps us farmers and ranchers on our toes. We shoot 'em, so we do. Threat to our livelihood. There's plenty more where those two come from."

Mary's heart sank. She eyed the black dog.

"Well, tell Art—Arthur, I mean—I appreciate his concern, but I do not want a dog. Not now, not ever."

"Huh. So you don't want a dog. Sorry, but I thought you did. Because Art said . . ." His voice drifted off when Mary broke in.

"Yeah, well, Art doesn't know. He had no right to think I would be interested in a dog."

Bob backed to the door, snapped his fingers, and with a hasty, "Evenin' ma'am," disappeared out the door with the dog.

Mary waited till the diesel truck rounded the corner at the bottom of the slope before throwing on a coat and parading out to the newly installed telephone in the wood house, dialing Arthur's number, and leaving him a frosty message.

Arthur listened to it, then smiled, finally laughed, and told Bob the following day that her message was so cold it about froze the phone to his ear. She was something, that Mary. Independent as all get out. Bob said most old maids were fiercely set in their ways. Let her find out for herself.

The visit from Bob only intensified Mary's fear. Small beads of sweat appeared on her upper lip as she pinned her black cape to her dress. She bit down on her teeth while she pinned the belt of her apron, rolling her eyes in the direction of the schoolhouse as she spooned up her oatmeal.

Well, what did Bob know? How often were humans attacked? She should have asked him. Her chances of being attacked were very slim. Or so she hoped. When she closed and locked the door of her house behind her, she took a deep, steadying breath. Straightening her shoulders, she set off down the steps, the wooden bat firmly in hand.

It was a beautiful early winter morning, the wind chasing little puffs of snow from wires and branches and uncovering some of the brown weeds by the road. It was cold, Mary thought, bending her head to the frigid air.

The twigs bent and snapped and branches swayed, but Mary refused to give in to her fear. The dogs would not be out and about if it was this cold. A distant barking sound increased the speed of her footsteps, so by the time she reached the porch of the small brown schoolhouse, her chest hurt by the force of her exertion. Whew!

Hurriedly, she put the bat back into the plastic garbage can, then began her day. There was no use letting that bit of information circulate among the community, now was there?

She had a good forenoon, the dogs forgotten, her head filled with lessons, teaching, and dealing with problems, the way she had done for twelve school terms before this one.

The children made construction paper turkeys for Thanksgiving, along with colorful horns of plenty. They copied a good poem about being thankful and planned a Thanksgiving dinner at school for the parents and members of the school board.

As the afternoon shadows lengthened once more, and the hands of the clock moved toward three o'clock, a sick feeling of dread gripped Mary's stomach. She tried hard to throw it off by becoming relaxed and nonchalant and trying to laugh with her pupils, but her mouth became dry, and she had to lick her lips repeatedly in order to speak.

When the school van approached, she almost stopped the driver and asked him to take her home, but she put her pride firmly in place before she actually did.

After the last "See ya!" had been sung out and the last children clambered on board the van and the buggies, she closed the door and shivered with genuine fear yet again. In a way, this was ridiculous. Tentatively, she touched the tips of her fingers to the scars on her face, sometimes angry and red, other times, barely visible.

The remembering is what it was. She could still smell the dogs' mouths and feel the overpowering strength of their bodies and their jaws. Suddenly, with an urge so powerful it left her drained, she wanted to go home. She'd promised Mam she'd be home for Christmas. Perhaps she'd be home for Thanksgiving.

She missed all the traffic and waving to people she knew. How she would appreciate the safety of the traffic! She'd count herself forever fortunate to wave to the folks she recognized and even the ones she didn't. The safety of those well-traveled roads was a longing so intense, Mary felt weak. Well, as she'd told herself before, self-pity was a well-traveled road to misery, and there was no use wanting something you could not have.

She bundled up and set off resolutely for the buggy shed to retrieve the bat she mentally labeled "The Guardian." She was just lifting it from the hiding place when the sound of buggy wheels made her drop the wooden bat like a hot coal. Straightening her back, she stood, then began to walk toward the schoolhouse.

It was Arthur Bontrager. Had he seen her lift the bat? Did he know she carried it around?

Arthur slid back the door of his top buggy, as these westerners called a buggy with a top. In Lancaster County, they were known as a *dochveggly*, literally meaning a "roof wagon." Whatever you called it, it was a form of transportation with sturdy wooden wheels that would convey her to her house, a few feet above the reach of the snapping jaws of stray dogs.

She wanted to throw herself in Arthur's arms and weep like a small child that is dreadfully afraid of the dark. What she did do, though, was watch his face warily with a timid smile of apology. There was that small matter of the phone message to deal with.

"Hey!"

"Hello!"

"I thought you might appreciate a ride home."

"Not unless you were going that way."

"What if I'm not?"

"I'll walk."

"All right, then."

Arthur's eyes crinkled up, the laugh rolled out of his chest, and he chirruped to his horse, a fine black Dutch Harness.

"Wait!" All the terror welled up in Mary's chest, successfully suppressing the all-invasive pride, and she said very fast, "I do need a ride. It's late. I have a lot to do."

Once she was seated beside him, he gently put the woolen lap robe around her, patted her knee, and let the blue in his eyes twinkle at her. "You have a habit of leaving grouchy messages?"

Completely at a loss for words, she opened her mouth, then closed it again, finally saying only, "Go," jutting her chin in the direction of her house.

Again, he laughed. "So you don't want a dog?"

"No."

"But you know you'll have to have one soon. Or else I'll have to haul you to school and back. A pack of six dogs killed about half of Wes Owen's calves. Nice 500-pounders. There's a warning out for anyone walking or jogging."

Chapter Six

WAS IT SO WRONG FOR MARY TO MOVE ONLY A slight bit closer to Arthur in his top buggy after he had finished speaking?

Gratitude welled in her heart for his endless jolly laugh, his simple acknowledgement of forgiveness. She had been quite forthright, that she had.

She shivered. Instantly, he tucked the lap robe around her even more securely.

"Warm?"

"Scared."

"So you didn't like Bob coming with the dog? You know he raises those Bouvier des Flandres dogs. I think they're French or something."

"Boo-veay what?"

"Des Flandres."

"Never heard of them."

"I think they are an extraordinary breed. I would love to see one lying by your woodstove."

"But. . . ."

"I know. You don't like dogs."

"I really don't."

"You don't like men who try to make you own one, either."

"Well . . ."

His laugh rang out.

Mary was genuinely sorry to see that they had already reached her house. Now she would be alone again.

"There you are," Arthur said, pulling back on the reins, turning the buggy wheels slightly to the right. Then, to tease her, he asked, "What's for supper?"

Mary stepped down and reached under the seat for her book bag and lunchbox. A thought pulsed through her head. She weighed the cold and the loneliness, the homesickness and fear of her walk to school, versus Arthur's face, his laugh, his big, solid strength that made a house warm and secure.

"I was thinking of making shoofly pie tonight. I have some rice and chicken I was going to make into soup."

"Do you mind very much if I invite myself for the shoofly pie? I have often heard of it but never tasted it."

"No, you can help. Or, I mean, I'll cook supper." Flustered, losing efficiency, she stumbled.

"Be right back." He drove home in record time, and Mary changed clothes because he had never seen her wear this mint green dress. She combed her hair, telling herself it didn't matter if she was a bit disheveled, and brushed her teeth because she always brushed them when she got home from school. Well, at bedtime, anyway.

Her cheeks were red, her freckles danced across her nose in anticipation, but she told herself that to-night she would ask him in complete honesty about the girl in the photograph at his house. She would finally do it.

All evening she planned on it. When she measured the all-purpose flour, Crisco, soda, and salt, when she mixed the pie dough with her hands and rolled it out with the wooden rolling pin, she meant to ask him. She spooned out brown sugar, counted eggs, and measured molasses, hot water, and baking soda. Arthur mixed the crumbs—the flour, brown sugar, and butter for the top of the pie—and all that while she truly meant to ask about the girl.

When the three pie crusts were rolled out perfectly, the wet ingredients divided among the unbaked crusts, the crumbs piled high on top, and the full pies put carefully into the oven, Mary's small house was filled with the wonderful aroma of baking molasses and brown sugar and pie dough.

She made a delicious chicken rice soup, and they ate it with chunks of good Swiss cheese, olives, and homemade Lebanon bologna she had shipped from home. She heated leftover dinner rolls and melted pats of butter across their tops. Arthur had laughed at Mary when she said she was just simply going to give up and make a sandwich. Arthur said he'd love to have some applesauce, that he always cooled his soup with saltines and applesauce, if that was okay.

She meant to ask him after the pies were finished baking and taken from the oven. She really did.

After the pies had cooled, she cut each one into fourths, then served him a wedge on one of her Corelle dishes. She sat down, watching his face eagerly as he took the first bite. She smiled when he savored it slowly, then giggled like a bashful schoolgirl when he rolled his eyes and said it was the best thing he'd ever eaten.

Even if it was an eight-inch pie, it was a bit frightening that he ate the whole thing. But then she guessed chicken rice soup was not very filling for a man his size, even with saltines and applesauce.

The house was warm from the oven's heat, as well as the crackling woodstove. Arthur chewed on a toothpick as he washed dishes at the small sink, leaving no room for her to dry them. He was so slow. His hands were so big they almost filled the sink. He added far too much dish soap and didn't rinse them clean enough, but Mary didn't say anything. She waited politely till he was done washing, then slipped into the small sink alcove, dried the dishes quickly, and put them away.

He sat on the sofa, dwarfing it. She stood uncertainly, aware of her size nine shoes, her hands hanging awkwardly by her sides. He said he hated the thought of going home. Mary blushed but busied herself back at the sink rearranging dish towels absentmindedly. She would ask him now.

Arthur looked out the window behind the couch and said he believed it was snowing. Then, because it was so unbearably cozy and lovely to have him here, with the snow falling on the roof and the edges of the porch, and the smoke from the woodstove reaching up through the tiny snowflakes into the cold and the dark and the wind, she knew she could not do this again. She was not going to make a habit of entertaining someone else's man.

So she said very loud and clear, "Well, it's my bedtime."

"Are you asking me to leave?"

"Yes."

"Really? Don't you want to play a game of Upwords?"

"Upwords? You play Upwords?"

"I do."

"I don't know one man who enjoys that game."

"Well, now you do."

They brought out the card table and set up the plastic board game. Each reached for seven tiles and the game began.

Mary's competitive streak bordered closely on poor sportsmanship, which made Arthur chuckle constantly, inflaming her temper. When he won by quite a wide margin, she said it was because it was her bedtime and she had asked him to leave and he didn't. She was tired and not thinking right.

He got up and prepared to leave, still smiling. She could not bear to see him go, so she said if he wanted, she'd make him a cup of coffee. He watched her face quizzically and asked why.

"Well, I . . ." Then she stopped.

He waited.

Headlong without thinking, she dived into the turbulent waters of the unknown. "Arthur, I'm guilty."

"Of what?"

"I feel as if I shouldn't be spending these evenings with you. It's not right."

"What are you talking about?"

She was too ashamed to tell him, too ashamed to stop midway.

"I know you'll think less of me, but you must know this. I picked up a photograph of . . . of your friend. Your girlfriend."

Miserably, she hung her head. There were her feet, as big and obnoxious as always. Oh, why had she even started this? What made her think Arthur ever harbored any feelings for her?

Slowly, Arthur breathed out. All the creases in his eyes disappeared, and they became large and sad and very dark blue.

What he said, was, "Bring the coffee to the living room," and went to sit at one end of the sofa, his eyes unfathomable, brooding.

So now he was angry. She had done something so grievously wrong that his good-natured laugh was silenced to this moody stillness.

Quietly, Mary placed a mug of coffee on a coaster at his elbow. Softly, she sat at the opposite end of the couch, clinging to the rounded, brown arm. She lifted the mug silently to her lips, her eyes averted, unable to watch the great change in his face any longer.

"Mary, I don't have a girlfriend. Only a memory of her."

Mary waited. The snow pinged against the windowpane. The wind rattled the loose trim on the corner of the small house.

"I guess that explains your strange behavior," Arthur said gruffly.

Mary stared at her shoes. His girlfriend had told him off and broken the relationship, and he would never love again. Some men were like that.

"Well," Mary justified herself.

"No need to explain. I understand. Absolutely."

"I don't want you to think that I am thinking of you in a . . . uh . . . you know." Mary spread her hands, a great painful blush hiding her freckles. She was glad for the wan light from the kitchen. Then, because she did not know what to do or say, she got up, went to the refrigerator, opened the milk bottle and poured more milk into her coffee cup. She stirred it busily, her eyes lowered.

Arthur remained quiet, watching her.

When no words were forthcoming, Mary realized his kind heart, and since she believed he did not want to hurt her, he said nothing at all.

She knew, also, that by speaking to him in that fashion, she had shamelessly thrown herself at his feet. And he did not want her. He had never spoken to her in any romantic way or shown that he was remotely attracted to her. His kindness, that gentleness that radiated from him, was all he felt for her. It was the same feeling he had for every single person who knew him.

An obstruction built in her throat, the beginning of her defeat that would evolve into a sob, the epitome of weakness. Swallowing, she drew up the emotional shield she used so handily to protect the matters of her heart. She sat back down on the couch.

"Arthur, I was thinking of going home for Thanksgiving. I think this evening helped me to make up my mind. I will go home. I have failed here and been mauled by wild dogs, and I want to go back to Pennsylvania. I miss my parents, my way of life. I'm going back. I can never make it here." She was babbling now, a sort of incoherence flavoring her words with panic.

"You didn't allow me to finish my story."

"Well, Arthur, that's all right. You don't have to finish it. I know what you want to say, but you don't have to. I understand."

He rose from the couch and stood directly in front of her. Then he did something so alarming, so completely out of his character, that Mary gasped. He lowered his face and put a hand over her mouth.

"Be quiet. You're not making any sense at all."
Mary sat back.

"Oh, you!" Her fingers clenched into fists as she let the anger and hurt, the disappointment and remorse blaze from her eyes. "Just go home, Arthur. Go home and leave me alone. I was perfectly all right before this. I could always manage my life on my own."

"You did not give me time to explain about the photograph. You've been so busy telling me you're going home, that you have everything under control."

"Well, I do—have everything under control, I mean."

She was surprised when Arthur began to laugh.

"Yes, you do, Mary. You always do. Only your life is a mess where one thing is concerned. But the time to explain that to you is not now. So I'll go home. I'm bringing the dog tomorrow evening. I don't have time to bundle you back and forth every day to and from school."

He got his big, black corduroy coat down from the hook by the doorway and shrugged into it.

"I don't want that dog!" Mary screeched.

Arthur said very firmly, "You're getting him though. If you don't, your life is in danger."

He closed the door with a firm click.

Mary yanked the door open and called after his retreating figure, "I am going back home!"

He kept walking, spreading his hands and lifting his shoulders in an expression of complete nonchalance.

Oh, he made her so angry! She stepped back and gave the door a good hard slam.

Sure enough, the following evening, after she had made two terrifying walks to and from school, the dog arrived. He could be clipped, Bob explained. It would alter his appearance, but then she could see his eyes.

Mary nodded tersely, her mouth a thin line of distaste. She acknowledged the dog's presence by a mere look, then went to get her checkbook. Bob held out his hands, palms in front of him, and explained that the payment was taken care of. He wasted no time walking to his truck, turning it around and rattling away.

Mary inserted one forefinger somewhere around the region of the dog's neck, tentatively exploring for a collar. She came up with one made of intricate braided leather.

"Well, dog, I hope you like woodsheds, because that is where you'll be," she said, hoping he understood the efficiency with which she rid herself of Arthur and fully planned to do with him.

He would be a sort of mechanical dog to her. A robot. Eat food and drink water. Live in shed. Walk to school. Protect teacher.

"Come on."

Immediately, the obedient dog followed her to the door of the woodshed, stood patiently while she opened the door, then trotted inside, sniffing the ground floor, the pieces of bark scattered about, the rich smell of wood and sawdust.

"Here you are, dog. Your new home."

The only thing that made Mary feel bad was the biting cold. If he was a house dog, he'd freeze out here. She went to the house, debated a long time, but finally chose the knotted flannel comforter her mother had given her. She did not like the dog, but cruelty to animals was another category entirely.

When she reappeared, the dog took a step forward, as if asking permission to enter the house.

"No. This is your domain, dog. Outside. Out."

She placed the comforter on the wooden floor, flinched at the cold shed, placed his food and water a comfortable distance away, and commanded, "Lie down." The dog gave her a long look, at least that's what it felt like he was doing, then lay down obediently. She got out quickly, latching the door firmly.

She got ready for bed, first enjoying a hot shower and then a cup of hot chocolate, and felt only a twinge of guilt. This is Montana, dog. Grow up. You'll run me to school, so you'll get warmed up.

She went to bed, lost herself in the deep mound of warm covers, shifted to a comfortable position, and lay sleepless.

Of course he was warm enough, she told herself. He'd bark if he got too cold. But what if he was shivering? Cold was so harsh, so cruel. Suppose he was out there crying? Would she hear? Finally she got up, pulled on a pair of boots, clasped her bathrobe around her waist and ventured out to the woodshed.

When she opened the door, the beam of her flashlight found the big dog lying on top of the comforter, shivering uncontrollably.

"Dog!" Mary exclaimed. She was so upset. She had never planned to be cruel.

She had a notion to go right up the hill to Arthur and deliver the dog right back to him. The thought of her morning walk to school was the only thing that changed her mind.

So what was she to do? Having everything under control meant doing things her way. She did not want to give in to letting a dog—and a big, black, hairy one at that—into her clean house.

Going to the dog, she bent over and gave him a small push. If only he'd crawl between the folds of the comforter, he'd warm up. "Get off, dog. Up. Get up!"

Mary lifted a corner of the blanket. The dog rose, shivering miserably. He stood uncertainly, then laid down again on top of the comforter.

"Stupid dog. Then just be cold."

Mary went back to bed, telling herself he would get warm by himself. But she slept fitfully and woke up tired with a pounding headache above one eye that lasted all day.

The schoolchildren made such a fuss that Mary had a hard time restoring order. They petted the dog, they clipped the hair away from his eyes, they braided some of the hair on his tail and told her he had to have a name.

Blackie. Fred. Barney. Leo. Sam.

Finally, Mary said they could each write one name on a slip of paper, then put them all in a box and she would draw one. It was the only fair way she knew to do it.

Sam. That was the name written on the paper that Mary chose, so Sam he was.

Mary strode home, the dog on a leash, trotting by her side. She could see his eyes now, as black as his hair, inquisitive, searching the roadside, lifting his nose to any new or unusual scents.

It was worrisome, the amount of dog food she'd need. Where in this remote county did one go about procuring dog food? She knew how far away the closest Walmart was, and she couldn't pay around a hundred dollars for dog food at one time.

She left Arthur a terse message, and he left her one a few hours later. "The feed man will deliver it for you, Mary. Here's their number. Have a good evening." So typical of him. Didn't that man have a mean bone in his body? He was as guileless as a sheep.

So she ordered dog food and fought with herself about Sam's sleeping accommodations. When the wind moaned around the edges of the house, Mary peered at the thermometer attached to the window. Surely not five degrees and falling! It was barely the end of November. Well, she could not leave the dog by himself in the shed. That was all there was to it. But she could not let him sleep in the house without a bath either.

Grimly, she opened the door to find Sam cowering beneath the rustic porch chair, his black coat powdered with a dusting of windblown snow, shivering again. Holding the door wide, Mary said, "Come on, Sam."

The big dog raised himself to his feet, looked at Mary quizzically, then trotted past her into the small kitchen. Never hesitating, he went straight to the woodstove and lay down beside it.

"No, dog—I mean, Sam—you can't do that."

She spent the rest of the evening getting him into the small bathtub and persuading him to stay there, then using half a bottle of shampoo with a scrub brush, and finally half-drowning the sorrowful creature with a rinse from the shower.

The bathroom floor was soaked, and Mary's dress and apron were sodden. She had used two whole towels to dry all that hair, and he still smelled like a dog.

Mary sighed, knowing she could not put herself through that again. Sam was as clean as he was ever going to be.

She checked the area around the stove for stray dog hair but saw none. She almost got out her small gold magnifying glass to make sure, then decided against it. That was too overboard, as her pupils would say.

Sam explored the small house and examined each corner, sniffing at chairs and rugs and the small refrigerator set into the oak cupboards. When he licked a spot on the linoleum, Mary scolded him, saying, "No, Sam, don't do that." She opened a drawer and pulled out an old rag, wet it with soap and water, then rubbed vigorously.

Dogs were just not pleasant things to have in the house. She scoured the bathtub with Clorox bleach twice before she had her shower, searching everywhere for signs of hidden dog hair.

She spread an old rug by the door and set the dog food and water on it. She figured she could wash it every week, as she certainly could not put up with dog slobber, now, could she?

Sam settled down by the stove and closed his eyes. Outside, the wind shifted the snow into uneven drifts. The cold crept around the corners of the house, and Sam laid his massive head on his paws that had been washed with shampoo and conditioner, as he watched his new mistress with sad eyes.

Sam marked his territory around the small house, the roadside, and the schoolhouse, the way dogs do. And when the pack of wild dogs came near, they swerved around it, a small but meaningful obstacle on their way to slaughtering more animals.

Mary lay sleeping, unaware of the way of nature and dogs. She had come to the conclusion that it was a very good thing she was going home, rather than having to live with this dog she had no feelings for. The same went for Arthur.

Bossy man.

Chapter Seven

THE THANKSGIVING GET-TOGETHER AT SCHOOL
was long anticipated, the children eager to give their
parents a tour around the classroom, showing their
artwork and stories they had written. Mary had
baked eight shoofly pies. That was her contribution
to the many dishes that would arrive.

She dressed carefully, wearing brown, which she
thought was a Thanksgiving color. She paid special
attention to her hair and wore her new, white Sunday
covering.

She loaded the pies onto the sled in a cardboard
box tied down with a piece of string, got into her
coat and boots, pulled on her gloves, and looked at
Sam. *Ach*, she'd leave him at home. He'd be under-
foot, sniffing at the food and getting in the way, and
she was pretty sure there were plenty of mothers who
did not want a big black dog in the classroom.

Sam rose, eager for the leash. He bounced playfully,
then held his head to one side, unable to understand.

"Stay, Sam."

He whined softly.

"*Ach,* you're spoiled. Well, you'll have to stay in the shed at school."

Sam trotted ahead while Mary pulled the sled with one hand, looping the leash around the other.

The air was gray and heavy, the atmosphere damp and bone-chilling. She should have worn a bonnet, but it would have smashed her new covering.

With Sam to accompany her, Mary no longer watched the line of brush and trees or the surrounding countryside. She felt protected, trusting Sam to keep her safe, so it was a bit of a shock to feel the leash in her hand go slack.

Sam stopped. Mary's eyes moved from left to right. The old fear rose in her chest, suffocating her till she fought down the panic-stricken feeling.

"What, Sam?" Sam stood erect, his forelegs perfectly aligned, his back legs bent powerfully, his ears lifted.

Mary felt the scream forming and lost all sense of reason when she saw the low, undulating line of movement behind the grove of aspens to her right.

"No! No! Oh please, God, no!"

She dropped the string attached to the sled, then turned and ran blindly, slipping and sliding, falling, getting back to her feet, and sobbing hysterically.

Sam could not hold off the entire pack. What had Bob said? Six of them?

She ran on. She stepped on hidden ice, her knee hitting a rock as she went down hard. Pain exploded through her leg, but she rose to her feet and kept going.

Through the panic, she caught sight of her house. Would she make it before the dogs overtook her? The thought of jaws tearing at her flesh spurred her on. Her lungs were flames of pain, her breath coming in short spurts. Her ribs ached, but her feet kept pounding down on the snow.

She threw herself on the small brown porch, then turned to see if Sam had followed. Why wasn't he barking? Oh, the vicious dogs would tear him to pieces. She had deserted him, too selfish to think of anything but herself. It had been her only thought. Poor, poor Sam.

She listened. In the distance, the baying of the dogs could be heard plainly. Mary gripped the porch post, hanging onto it as tears of gratitude rained down her face. *Denke, Herr. Denke.*

Immediately, a sense of terrible shame came on her. Sam would be torn apart. He'd be bait for them. Should she try and go to him? Or call Arthur?

The baying sound remained the same, rising and falling. Why didn't Sam bark? Had they already killed him? Sam was large and powerful, but no dog could outlast six others, especially not these seasoned killers.

Unsure, Mary stayed by the porch post, watching, listening. She heard a buggy rattling by and saw Arthur's black horse. Oh, now he'd find the sled and the pies. What if the dogs had gotten Sam? Heartsick, Mary went inside, dropped onto a kitchen chair, then got up and flung open the door, as if she could see Arthur's approach.

What should she do? The parents and schoolchildren would be arriving, and she was not there. Well, this was a situation that called for calm measures, so the first thing was to realize that she was safe. And thankful. The second thing was the fact that she did care very much about Sam, which was fortunate, since she'd be here till Christmas, now that she'd decided to stay for Thanksgiving.

Oh, what was this? Sam!

"Oh, Sam! Come on, boy! Get up here! Come on!" Mary yelled, slapping her knees, then lowering herself to hug the cold, panting dog. She clung to his neck, smelled the dog smell of his black coat, and thought it didn't smell nearly as bad as she always thought.

"Good dog! Good, brave, wonderful dog!" She followed him inside and fed him a few slices of her best ham, the kind that cost $5.99 a pound at the Amish bulk food store. "Sam, you drove them off! You did!"

Sam gobbled up the ham, his eyes holding an expression of dog joy, as Mary bent to kiss the top of his head. She told him again what a brave dog he was. She took off her coat and her covering and went to the bathroom to fix her hair. Red strands had come loose and hung sloppily over her forehead.

Ugh. Sometimes it would be nice to have a different view in the mirror. Always those freckles, topped by the carroty hair. Her hands were too unsteady to draw the fine-toothed comb through it, so she sat down on the edge of the tub and took a steadying breath.

Would Arthur find the shoofly pies? The sled? It was all right that he wouldn't care. She had accepted the fact that his heart belonged to the memory of the girl in the photograph. She would be going home for Christmas, perhaps to stay. She planned on making the announcement at school after the Thanksgiving dinner was eaten.

She combed her hair, then set the new white covering carefully on top, tied it neatly, and turned to leave the bathroom, when the door leading to the porch was yanked open from outside. Mary gasped when Arthur Bontrager stood in the doorway, his face as white as chalk, calling "Mary!" in a terrible voice.

"Oh, my! What is it, Arthur?"

When he caught sight of her, his shoulders dropped as relief washed across his features. Color followed immediately, and quick tears made the ice blue diamonds in his eyes shimmer.

"Mary! There you are."

"What happened?"

"I came on the sled in the middle of the road, that's what happened. You or your dog were nowhere about. What was I supposed to think?" His voice was hoarse with emotion, his face working.

"Well, my goodness," Mary said, coolly.

"Oh, okay, Mary. You can stand there and say that. You have no idea what it's like when you care about someone, now, do you?"

What had gotten into him? This was Arthur? Laughing, easygoing Arthur? Oh, it was the dog, Sam. He'd paid two thousand dollars for him. Well, of course he cared about Sam.

"Arthur, Sam is okay. He held off the dogs, I think."

"What dogs?"

"The dogs. The pack of six. They were off a ways to the right behind that grove of aspens. I sort of lost my common sense and ran. I ran home. But Sam came soon afterward. I mean, of course you care. You paid a lot of money for him."

Arthur lowered his head to wipe his shoes on the rug inside the door. Two steps and he confronted Mary. He placed his large heavy hands on her shoulders and said in a gruff voice barely above a whisper, "I didn't mean Sam, I meant you. You, Mary. I care very much what happens to you."

His eyes never left her startled, wide green ones. As the color left her face, her brown freckles stood out in stark contrast.

Arthur lifted his hand, touched her freckled nose, lightly, and said, barely above a whisper, "Someday, I want to kiss every one of your freckles. But since you are who you are, I can wait." Instantly, his mood changed. He became lighthearted, bantering like the old Arthur she knew.

She put on her coat, her feet firmly encased among clouds. Stardust flipped and somersaulted through the air when she lifted her arms to button her coat. She almost fainted with the beauty of his words as she bent to put on her boots. When she straightened and Arthur looked into her eyes, she heard the strains of the singing she had always longed for and never found.

The Thanksgiving get-together went very well. The parents, all seven pairs of them, plus Arthur, brought so much food, the ping-pong table in the center of the room groaned with weight.

The brown paper turkeys and orange pumpkins on the wall, the poetry the children recited, the songs they sang, were all very festive. John Weaver read a special story about the Indians and Pilgrims, causing a few of the women to weep openly.

Mary moved among the people, held babies, complimented the mothers' cooking, and felt very much a part of them. Here she was, the owl among pigeons, with her heart-shaped covering and her black apron, but now there was a difference. She was an accepted owl, an honored one, she might add. She felt her place in the community keenly. She was a necessary item, part of the wheel that kept everyone together. The ministers were the hub of the wheel, but she was one of the bolts that kept the spokes intact.

She was a teacher and a good one. She knew that. She knew a problem school sometimes lacked the voice of experience. Most folks were good-hearted, temperate, if you worked in love and understanding.

When Kenny Yoder came up to her and shook her hand, his narrow face beaming with kindness, Mary faced him squarely, taking his hand firmly. "You know, I really don't know how you do it. I have never heard my boys say they like school, and certainly not the teacher. You're amazing. They must train teachers in Lancaster."

"Oh, no. We have our share of problems. I've been a teacher for twelve years and learned by trial and error." They were interrupted by his wife, Ella Mae, a thin hawkish woman who always scared the daylights out of Mary.

"Thank you, Mary, for the good dinner."

"Wasn't me!" Mary laughed.

Ella Mae smiled. "Thank you, too, for what you do for the boys."

Flowery words of praise followed, falling easily on Mary's accepting ears. My goodness, this was the problem couple?

She tapped the small bell to get everyone's attention, then made her announcement in a clear, precise tone. She was going home for Christmas, perhaps to stay. A chorus of disbelief, a proclamation of denial, began as a murmur, then rose and swelled around her until she dropped her shoulders, raised her eyebrows, and lifted her hands in a questioning gesture.

Dave Troyer stood up. "Hey, the captain never leaves his ship."

Paul Weaver rose to his feet. "Come on, Mary. What is it? More pay? Homesick? The cold? What it is, we'll fix it."

Mary laughed, hiding the real reason from prying eyes. No, they could not fix her dilemma. For almost an hour, Mary had believed Arthur's startling words, but then she began her usual train of negative thoughts until she convinced herself that Arthur was a flirt. He didn't want her. No man ever had, no man ever would. How could they? She was nothing. Her feet were huge and flat and white, and they even had a few freckles on them. Her arms were too long and skinny, her hands big and ungainly, her hair red as fire, the freckles the sparks from it.

Many times, Mam had told her that looks has nothing to do with it. Huh-uh, Mam. Looks do have something to do with it. How many times had she been attracted to young men, even the homeliest, the least popular, and never once had one of them asked the question? Always, always, they turned to normal looking young girls with brown hair or black. With nice figures and small feet and personalities that entertained them.

She had prayed for fifteen years. She firmly believed that God controlled matters of the heart. He wrote our faith, like an author, and He finished the story, just the way the Bible said. So, it was ultimately up to God, and Mary finally figured out that she was meant to be alone.

Why, other than red hair and unfortunate freckles, was she alone? Because God wanted her to be. That was why. So Arthur Bontrager would just have to go fly a kite.

She steadied her shoulders, dipped her head, acknowledged the praise and the begging to stay, but her eyes shimmered with unshed tears, and never once did she acknowledge Arthur's presence. She knew where he was sitting, when he moved, how easily he talked and laughed, how he was the center of attention so much of the time.

The children crowded around her after the announcement. Little Lila Mae, the first-grader, hugged Mary hard, lifted her sweet face with blue eyes as guileless as—okay, as guileless as Arthur's—and lisped, "Right, Teacher, it's not true? You'll go home for Christmas, but you'll be back? Right?"

Mary drew the little girl onto her lap, hugged her, held her sweet body against her own, and whispered, "I'll tell you a secret, if you don't tell anyone else."

Eagerly, Lila Mae nodded.

"I'm going home for Christmas. Then when I'm there, I'll see how I feel. I'll pray long and hard so God can show me the way."

"Good idea." Satisfied, she strained against Mary's arms, slid off her lap, and went to join her classmates.

Alone in the schoolroom, the afternoon fading to evening as the steel-gray turned darker by the minute, Mary hummed as she swept the floor. She smiled as she got down the dust pan and brush and whistled softly as she dumped the dirt into the trash can.

She was going home! Four more weeks, and she'd be home for Christmas. The phone calls and letters she received were only a stand-in, barely sufficient to stave off her homesickness. Now she could count the days, marking the calendar with big Xs like a child.

Her walk home was uneventful with Sam trotting obediently by her side, the leash coiled and lying on the sled. Neither of them needed it. This faithful dog was so loyal, it was almost pitiful.

Mary did keep her eyes trained on the road ahead of her to hold the fear and panic at bay. She realized Sam would stop if there was danger. Repeatedly he would dash into the brush, then back out. She'd never seen a dog who had to relieve himself so much. Maybe he had a kidney disease. She'd have to ask Arthur. He'd know. Or, she wouldn't, on second thought. She would not have Arthur in her life at all. It was far easier.

On Thanksgiving Day she was alone. There was no school. She slept late, stretched luxuriously, and put a small chicken in the oven that she had stuffed with cornbread stuffing. She ate a huge breakfast of pancakes, sausage, and scrambled eggs. She wished she had orange juice, but in these parts, if you were out of something, you were simply out of it. If you wanted orange juice, you had to have the good sense to buy frozen concentrate.

She sipped her coffee, then moved to the living room. When Sam rose to follow her, she tried not to wince, but tried instead to convince herself that he really did not shed dog hair all over her house. He didn't smell like a dog. Well, not much anyway. And he was a good companion. Mary reached down to ruffle his ears and was rewarded with a look of total and absolute devotion.

"Good Sam. Good dog," Mary said softly, then looked around, feeling silly for giving her love and praise to a dog. It was so not her.

When the chicken was tender, she made gravy and opened a can of beans. She didn't feel like peeling, cooking, and mashing potatoes. She was hungry for baked beans, so she ate them with the chicken, made a cup of tea, and then flopped on the recliner to read *The Connection*. When she fell asleep after a few pages, Sam laid his head on his paws and closed his eyes as well.

Outside, the snow finally began to fall. The world around the primitive little cabin turned from a white gray to a gray that was steadily overtaken by darkness, so when the snow began to drift down, no one knew unless they were outside. It was a deep, quiet night, the snowflakes whispering softly as they fell to the ground, covering the aspens, the pines, and cedars.

When Mary awoke, the clock's hands pointed to the seven and nine. Dark already, she thought, and not yet seven o'clock. Suddenly the evening stretched before her, long and cold and lonesome. A sense of melancholy wrapped itself around her like a smothering blanket, a feeling she did not understand. She felt almost like she had entered a void, reminding her of how parents and school board members often described the experience of a troubled child.

Sometimes the parents' misdeeds or their lack of caring created a void. Well, she'd certainly not suffered neglect from her family. She'd grown up in a world where she never questioned her parents' absolute love and concern.

She'd just take care of this senseless depression immediately and get herself to work. The foot rest of the recliner slapped down, startling Sam, who leaped to his feet, eyeing Mary uncertainly. She ignored him and went to her desk to get her pale blue stationery and her best black ink pen. Then she hustled to the small kitchen table, took off the pen's cap, put it on the opposite end of the pen, but instead of writing, began to chew on it. Who would she write to?

She had spoken to her mother and to Rachel yesterday. Liz was too wrapped up in her wedding plans. Good thing Elam didn't want to get married till spring. Otherwise, she'd have to go to Pennsylvania in November, when all the weddings, or at least half of them, took place.

Weddings. She always made a necessary appearance, but almost nothing in her life was harder, except perhaps a funeral. She was a master of deceit, she supposed. She listened to the sermon and was glad all day, happy for Elsie or Barbara or Anna or Rebecca. They each deserved a good husband.

Buried deep in her heart, she wondered how it would feel to stand beside a young man, hold his hand in front of the bishop, and pronounce the quiet, "*Ya*," that sacred promise to care for him in sickness and health, for richer or for poorer.

She would gladly have had any one of them. Reuben King was the first one she thought might ask her. He didn't. After he married her best friend, Sadie Zook, she figured probably Leroy Beiler would, the way he spoke to her whenever he had a chance. In the end, Leroy had used her to see if Edna Stoltzfus would go with him.

On and on, the story of her life. She accepted it now. But when sadness entered her life, could she honestly say there was no void? There wasn't supposed to be. God filled hearts and minds with His great unending love. Many girls were blessed beyond measure by staying single. Even the Apostle Paul said it was better to remain unmarried to serve the Lord more fully.

She knew some of the girls she was acquainted with wanted to remain single. But she honestly could not feel she was completely happy being single. But since when? She had been content in Lancaster County. She never thought much about men or marriage. Teaching fulfilled her, she believed.

Laying down her pen, she folded her thin arms on the table top and sighed. The soft hissing of the lamp faded away, then returned when she lifted her head and put up both hands to rest her chin in the cupped palms.

How hard would it be to leave Montana? She thought of never seeing Arthur Bontrager again and figured it was perfectly possible to leave Montana, knowing that meant she'd live the rest of her life without seeing him. She'd forget about him if she never heard his laugh. She'd forget his stubby nose and creases around his eyes. She'd forget all that nonsense he didn't even mean, like caring about her and. . . .

Well, now that was unthinkable, what he'd said about her freckles. She could feel the color suffuse her cheeks. *Ach*, I should not have come. I should have stayed home in good, old fast-paced Ronks, Pennsylvania. Out here there's too much time to think. The sky is too big and the mountains are too high and there is snow on top of them . . . the aspens turn yellow and the wolves howl and I want to live in Arthur's beautiful log house with all the windows that need to be washed.

For one instant she let the sweet truth fill her heart, but only for one instant.

Chapter Eight

MARY THREW HERSELF INTO HER SCHOOLWORK. The children were the fortunate recipients of every available skill she could muster. They studied for her pop quizzes, learned new Christmas songs, wrote their own poetry, and decorated the classroom with all the clever artwork they could create.

The snow was deep and beautiful, drifted high in some hollows and blown across windswept grades. The view from the schoolhouse was breathtaking—the pines, mountains, and vast, rolling acres of snow dotted with black cattle.

Mary and the schoolchildren decided that if a school Christmas play was so unpopular, they'd have an evening hymn sing. The children could recite poems if they wanted to, but they didn't need to. Everyone would sing together.

They'd finish with snacks—coffee and hot chocolate, Christmas cookies, homemade candy, snack mix, fruit desserts, and puddings, whatever families wanted to bring.

The children would wear red or green. They suggested Mary wear red, too. They were all seated around the woodstove eating their lunches and planning the Christmas festivities.

"No, I can't wear red!"

"Why not?"

Mary laughed. "I'd be red all over. Red hair, red freckles, red dress, red shoes."

"Not red shoes!" hooted little Andy, the second-grader.

"They'd shine red," Mary said.

"When do you have to go home?"

"Two days before Christmas. We'll have the Christmas singing and then I'll go back to my home near Lancaster."

"What does your house look like?"

"I already told you."

"Tell us again."

It seemed as if the children never tired of hearing about her life in Pennsylvania.

"Bet you didn't have a dog!" Betty, a seventh-grader, said.

"Oh, my goodness! Of course not!"

"Betty, she didn't need one."

"Nope. No wild dog packs in Ronks. They'd be smashed flat on the highway."

She had to explain about all the traffic again, then told the children she really didn't miss it anymore, but everyone went home for Christmas. That is what tradition required.

"But you're coming back, right?"

When Mary didn't answer immediately, the upper-graders raised their eyebrows. Betty giggled.

"What?" Mary asked sharply.

"You'll be back."

Why is it that children sometimes appear even more perceptive than adults? Mary had often experienced wise remarks coming from the sweet, guileless lips of a fifth-grader that put a situation in perspective. So, because she was afraid of where the covert glances would lead, and finding safety in the haven of denial, she dropped the subject.

On Sunday, she skipped church services because she had a bit of a headache and a scratch in her throat.

The wood fire was out at six o'clock that morning, the ashes gray and dead without one red spark. How irritating.

Mary slammed the cast iron door hard, shivered, then turned and leaped back into bed. Drawing the covers over her head, she coughed and went back to sleep.

A few hours later her nose felt much like an icicle, her hip hurt, and shivers chased themselves up her back and down her arms. She knew a fever was coming on. Good thing she decided to stay home from church. The room spun when she sat up, so she flopped back on the pillows, groaning.

She hoped Dave Mast got her message on their voicemail and wouldn't drive the extra miles to pick her up for church. But when she heard a sharp rapping sound on the door, she groaned again. Her head felt twice as big as it should be. The floor tilted to the right, then to the left, as she slung her heavy fleece bathrobe around her shoulders, slipped her feet into the ratty men's moccasins, and shuffled to the door.

Dismay grabbed her when she saw Arthur standing on the porch dressed in his Sunday suit, the heavy black wool overcoat making him appear even bigger. He filled the small, ramshackle porch.

Oh, no.

"Hey, Mary. Good morning."

Mary could not say anything. She was dumb-founded.

"I didn't see any smoke all morning and was afraid there was something wrong."

Mary shook her head.

Arthur asked if she was all right because her face looked flushed. She admitted she was coming down with the flu.

"Your fire's out, isn't it?"

"No. Well, yes, sort of." She just wanted him off that porch, in his buggy, and on his way to church.

"I can start the fire for you."

"No. You'll be late for church."

"You don't feel well at all, right?" he asked, leaning closer to look at her face. The dim morning light revealed flushed, feverish cheeks and two bright eyes.

"Just the flu."

"I'll start the fire."

"No. I can take care of myself."

When he knew she meant it, he said all right, then. Mary breathed a sigh of relief when he turned and left. She needed to barricade herself from him. He had no business knocking on her door, catching her unprepared, looking her worst with the flu and all.

She yelped in disbelief when she looked angrily in the mirror. Puffy eyes, brilliant freckles, white skin, cold sores breaking out on chapped lips, and her hair in the same despicable morning state it always was. The brilliant hue of her fleece bathrobe only served as a reflector to enhance the apparition that was her face.

She was sleeping in the recliner, covered with every cotton throw and fleece blanket she owned, when Arthur's knock interrupted her fitful dreaming.

Frightened and disoriented, she threw back the load of covers and was instantly assaulted by the cold air in the room. Shivering, her teeth chattered uncontrollably as she yanked open the door. She bit down hard on her lower lip to stop the trembling and peered at Arthur with feverish eyes.

"Mary, you are really sick."

When she shook her head, he grasped her shoulders and set her aside like an annoying piece of furniture. "I'm coming in."

Sam rose to meet him, his tail wagging, his eyes glad.

"How's it going, Sam? Huh?" Arthur dropped to his knees, ruffled the dog's ears, scratched his back, smoothed the thick black hair, and told him what a good dog he was, as Mary made her way back to the recliner and rolled herself back into all the blankets.

Arthur shrugged off his overcoat, rolled up the sleeves of his white shirt, opened the door of the woodstove, peered inside, and shook his head. The house was freezing, and there she was—very ill and as obstinate as ever.

He chopped kindling, crumpled newspaper, held a lighter to it, and was rewarded by a small flame that licked greedily at the dry kindling. He filled the red tea kettle, flicked on the burner, then looked at the pile of blankets that housed Mary somewhere in the middle.

He made a cup of comfrey tea, grilled a slice of bread in the skillet, spread butter on it, and walked to the recliner, bearing the lunch on a tray.

"Mary?" He said her name softly, like a question.

From deep beneath the covers, he heard a distinct, "Go away."

"I can't, Mary. You're very sick."

Suddenly, the covers were thrown back, and disheveled, shivering Mary emerged. Her eyes sparking angrily, and between chattering teeth, she spoke in halting words. "Yeah, I've been sick before. Just leave me alone. I'll be fine."

Arthur looked at the roaring stove. He walked over and shut the bottom door, latched it, threw on two chunks of split wood, clapped his hands to rid them of sawdust, and said to the wall, "You will not be fine."

Then he turned, his ice blue eyes wide, his annoyance turning them darker by the second. "I am not going away. I'm going to stay right here with you until you are able to be up and take care of this fire. It is my duty. So don't go off on a high horse saying how fine you are. You obviously aren't."

Holding the cup to her lips, he said, "Drink."

"Stop treating me like a child."

"Drink."

"My mouth hurts too much."

Bending, Arthur saw the painful blisters on both sides of her upper lip. He placed the palm of his hand on her forehead and gave a low whistle. He went into the bathroom and rummaged around, banging things, then emerged with a tube of cold sore medication, a bottle of Tylenol, and a hot water bottle.

She swallowed the pills obediently, applied the cold sore salve, then lay back and threw the covers over her head. When Arthur returned with the sloshing hot water bottle, he lifted the blankets from her head and asked if she was still breathing in there.

She glared at him, but when his eyes flattened, all the creases appeared in his tanned face, and his stubby nose widened, her glare turned to something softer. Her face showed insecurity. She was no longer safely within her circle of mustered up courage. A very small smile appeared, and she self-consciously lifted two fingers to hide the hideous blisters.

"Sit forward."

She obliged, and he slid the warm bottle behind her.

"Your lower back aches, doesn't it?"

"How do you know?" she snapped, angry that he would take the liberty of thinking he knew how she felt.

"Oh, flu does that. Makes your back hurt. Can you sit forward a bit more?"

He placed the hot water bottle on the exact spot that had caused her so much misery all morning. It was soft and warm and absolute bliss itself.

Arthur looked at the back of Mary's head and saw the great tangle of hair with hair pins nearly falling out, ready to disappear into the creases of the recliner. He couldn't help but notice how her thin shoulders shivered, her utter vulnerability, and he held very still. For an instant, he wondered what her usually severe bun of hair would look like, loosened and hanging around her shoulders.

Quickly, as if she read his thoughts, Mary sat back with her eyes closed, murmuring her thanks, a wan dismissal. "You can go now. I'll be all right."

He didn't say anything, just simply walked into the small kitchen, opened the refrigerator door, found the leftover Thanksgiving chicken and the broth, and set about making a pot of chicken noodle soup. He banged doors as he cooked, whistling soft and low and talking to Sam. He ate hard pretzels and slices of cheese as he worked, casting observant glances toward Mary who was once more rolled into the cocoon of blankets.

Arthur noticed the scented candles and the vase of pricey flowers that looked like silk or velvet. He observed her artwork, which wasn't cheap either. The cookware he was using was from Princess House. He raised his eyebrows. A high-class old maid. He smiled. Everything under control at all times. Yes, ma'am. He smiled again but turned quickly when the covers were flung back, the recliner groaning in protest as Mary sat up.

Reaching behind her back, she flung the hot water bottle across the floor. She kicked off the covers, lifted the handle that slapped the foot rest into place, and said she was burning up with that thing. She got to her feet and caught herself on the arm of the recliner, pushed off, then wobbled her way into the bathroom. Her face was flaming, her hairpins slithering out of the roll of hair on the back of her head.

Arthur noticed the frayed men's moccasins on her feet. Dear, funny Mary. He heard the shower while he searched for noodles. When he was unable to find some, he broke spaghetti into two-inch pieces, then

seasoned the dish with chicken base, poultry season-
ing, black pepper, and parsley. He glanced nervously
at the bathroom door.

He drank coffee, ate more pretzels, and finished
the cold baked beans he found in the refrigerator.
He thought the shower was running an awfully long
time.

He never knew anyone could be so proud, so self-
sufficient. She was something, Mary was.

The house had warmed up to a comfortable 72
degrees. Good. He added another stick of wood,
considered, then piled on two more. He'd make it
nice and warm.

The shower stopped.

Arthur ladled a bit of the soup into a bowl and
lifted the steaming liquid to his mouth for a taste.
He added a bit more salt to the soup in the kettle,
stirred, put the lid on, and turned the gas heat to the
lowest setting.

He noticed the stack of school books. A black,
well-worn Bible lay beside it, a blue and white journal
on top, the red Bic pen beside them. He would give a
fortune to know what lay between the covers of that

journal. Did this woman ever think about her single status? Did she ever consider being with someone? He doubted it. But then she made his world very interesting, presenting him with the challenge of his life.

When she finally emerged, her face and lips were chalk white, accentuated by the forest green of her dress. Her hair was rolled into a white towel thrown across the top of her head. She grasped a black hairbrush firmly in her right hand.

"Guess the Tylenol kicked in."

"Feel better?"

"Some." She sat on the sofa away from him. Lifting her hands, she unwrapped her hair and flung the towel across the back of a chair.

Arthur was not aware of the acceleration of his breathing. He just knew he would not allow her to see him watching her. Down came the dark, coppery tresses, parted in the middle, the weak, shaking hands resolutely drawing the brush through the gleaming mass.

Suddenly, she laid the brush hurriedly on the arm of the sofa and threw herself back against the cushions. "Whew! Weak as a kitten."

At least that's what Arthur thought she said. He got up, walked over to the sofa, and offered his assistance. He was turned down quite competently with an icy glare and a weak, "Of course not. I'm fine."

She picked up the brush and continued brushing. Arthur went back to the kitchen. He saw her draw the brush through the heavy wet hair, her profile etched against the wall. She turned her face, lifted her hair, clasped it behind her head, then resumed brushing. Arthur tried not to watch, he really did. From the moment he'd seen Mary, he found her mildly amusing, not beautiful, but a charming person with a sense of humor, smart, and quick with words.

He had never felt inferior to her, certainly not bashful or tongue-tied, the way young men often were when they became enamored of a girl. But now. Now he knew he was in awe of her. It was her complete and thorough misunderstanding of her own womanly charms that was so heartbreaking. It drew him with a powerful strength. He knew he was beginning to feel inferior and shy. He was bumbling, his breathing leaving him weak in the head. Even woozy. This was a turn of events.

Finally Mary lifted her hair completely unselfconsciously, as if she'd given up trying to be beautiful and accepted the fact that she was not enough for any man's eyes. Arthur felt waves of emotion. It was her too pure acceptance of being less than others that stirred him immensely.

When she spoke, he did not hear her. She turned, watched him, and still he was not aware. "Arthur."

He jumped. "Uh, yes, Mary?"

"You can go home now."

"Would you eat some of my chicken noodle soup?"

"I thought I smelled something good."

"Soup."

She walked to the kitchen, lifted the lid and sniffed, then replaced it. She turned and walked back to the table. He caught the scent of shampoo, soap, lotion, he didn't know what all. He knew one thing only—that not another day could go by until they talked of his past. He would stay right here until she listened to him.

She ate only a few spoonfuls of the soup. She said it was good, but she'd rather have another cup of tea. He almost dropped the tea kettle in his hurry to supply the hot, sweet drink. His hands shook when he spooned the sugar into the mug. He took a deep breath to steady himself.

He spent a large amount of time talking to Sam, who seemed happy with the undivided attention. Mary said she was feeling stronger, that it was getting on toward evening, and if he wanted to go back home to do chores, she really would be fine.

Arthur smiled at her. "How many times did you say you'd be fine?"

Mary kept her eyes averted, saying nothing. Quickly, then, she lifted her head and said, "I will be. You can go home and do chores."

"I'm afraid you'll let the fire go out again."

"I won't."

The silence that settled between them was painful, containing a new uncomfortable element, like a tic in an eye that has finally been acknowledged. Mary became unsure of herself, sensing something unusual in Arthur's face, in the way he looked at her. Perhaps it was her weakness or the effect of the Tylenol. She found it difficult to meet his eyes, or look at any part of his face, for that matter.

She drank her tea, put more salve on her cold sores, flicked the hair from her face. She coughed. Then, with the tension in the silence becoming unbearable, she said quickly, "Your shirt is so white."

"I learned how to do laundry from Miriam."

"Who is Miriam?"

When he did not reply, she picked up the mug of tea and drank quickly, with an unladylike slurp that was terrifying. "You don't have to tell me, if you'd rather not."

Arthur looked at Mary, his eyes filled with darkness, a color she had not known could possibly come from the usual light blue of his eyes that was like a diamond held to light. "Miriam was my wife."

Mary swallowed, cringing at the pain. "You . . . you had a wife?"

"I did."

A soft blush stole across Mary's face. She opened her mouth to say something, thought better of it, and closed it, incapable of speech.

"Although the girl in the photograph was my girlfriend, like I told you. First, I had Miriam. Then I dated Erma."

He let that information hang between them, a sword dangling dangerously on a thin thread, rife with the ability to sever, to maim, to hurt. Mary felt this so keenly she got to her feet, went to the double windows by the sofa, crossed her thin arms about herself, and lifted her eyes to the snowy hillsides and the pines surrounded by the majesty of the winter mountains.

Soon she'd go home for Christmas. She'd leave Arthur here in Montana with his unbearably twisted path of remembering. She was not capable of fixing his disappointments, his keenly felt losses. She wouldn't be able to lift his ton of memories. She couldn't begin to budge even one corner to allow him to be free.

Nor did she want to listen to him tell her all this. She stiffened when she heard him coming closer. She shrugged her shoulders when his hands clasped them. She stopped breathing when his hand lifted the heavy hair clasped firmly in the ponytail holder.

"Come, Mary, sit with me. We have all evening. If you feel well enough, you can hear my story."

"I don't want to."

"You don't?"

"No."

"May I ask why?"

"I can't. I don't know how to fix it."

"Oh, you're quite capable. You have it all under control."

She turned slowly, lifted her tired eyes still clouded with fever, and beckoned him to accompany her to the couch.

Chapter Nine

"MIRIAM WAS ONLY NINETEEN WHEN WE MARRIED. I was twenty-two. We lived in Indiana, one of the largest Amish settlements in the world. We were reasonably happy, but after four years of not being able to have children, Miriam was often unhappy and frustrated. I suppose I was, too. Another few years of—well, I'll just tell you, Mary—living in misery finally became a way of life.

"We went to doctors, tried gimmicks, especially anything labeled 'natural,' but nothing worked. I still wonder if Miriam's unhappiness was the root of her failing immune system. She was diagnosed with lymphoma, a deadly cancer, and died six months later." He stopped.

Mary whispered, "I am so sorry."

"Don't be. Our marriage was a burden. It took me years to recognize that sad fact. I always felt as if she didn't love me, and I really don't think she did. I'm not blameless either. My mistakes were many and frequent. I can't deny that.

"Her parents blamed me. Oh, they said they didn't, but I knew better. I came here to Montana. I made a lot of money in Indiana owning a stone mason company. I sold it, built my house here, and then lost most of my money running cattle."

He laughed suddenly, a deep rumbling release that brought back his usual good humor, which was a great relief to Mary. She wanted to throw herself into his arms and comfort him, but knew she had no power to do that. So she sat, her hands clasped in front of her primly, the way a red-haired, old-maid schoolteacher should.

"So, here I was, not rich, not poor, an ordinary guy who cooked and ate loads of good food to comfort himself and gained about a hundred pounds."

"You didn't!" Mary gasped.

"Almost."

Arthur's great laugh rang out freely as his face doubled up like an accordion. His teeth were very white in his tanned face, mirroring the white of his shirt.

Mary smiled, then she smiled wider, but the pain from the cold sores made her lift three fingers to press on them. And she stopped smiling.

"Those cold sores are mean, aren't they?" he asked, observing the way she touched them.

Mary nodded.

"So then Erma Miller came to Montana, looking for adventure, I guess. And being one of the eligible widowers and bachelors that tend to inhabit these parts, I tried to supply it. Looking back, she was too pretty, too fast, too spoiled. I was definitely not the one for her after a year or more. She told me so directly and hightailed it back to Ohio."

Mary watched Arthur shrewdly. She saw a flicker of regret, a painful confusion, but no real grief that weighed him down, as far as she could tell. But not so fast, she told herself.

"Actually, Mary, I should have known she was too much like Miriam, may she rest in peace. I did love her at first, passionately. She consumed me, filling every waking hour with her presence. I think in a way she replaced God, and I worshipped her. God seemed far away at that time. It's only since Erma left that I can truthfully say I have a close relationship with God, that I feel the warmth and protection of having Jesus Christ as my own

Redeemer. So I guess everything that happens in our lives has a reason."

Mary nodded, understanding.

"Erma left over four years ago, so I've pretty much accepted the solitude. I've even come to like it."

Dumbly, Mary nodded again.

"What's your story? There is surely a reason for someone like you to be alone."

For a long time Mary did not speak. When she did, her voice was low, stripped of any false courage or pride. "There is no story."

"Come on, Mary."

"Seriously, I'm ashamed to tell you. I have never been asked out on a date."

Arthur's eyes opened wide, the disbelief stamped all over his features. "I find that very hard to believe."

"Actually, you probably don't."

"What do you mean?"

"You know."

Bewildered, Arthur shrugged. Did Mary have some undisclosed, shameful past? He had to know. "Tell me."

She pointed to her freckles, her hair.

"It's this. As far as I can figure out."

"But, Mary, the color of your hair is the most attractive thing about you."

Completely uncomfortable with compliments of any kind, Mary spread her hands wide, clasped them across her knee, and shook her head in denial.

Arthur knew there probably had been a time when pale skin splattered with freckles was not his idea of beauty. The flawless, golden skin that Miriam possessed or Erma's tanned, smooth face was what he had thought attractive.

But love had many forms. The wonder, the beauty of it, was the way God provided the real love that would last. The love that sustained a person through valleys of tears and mountains of adversity. The way God led you to see the beauty of freckles and red hair and thin arms in one extremely confident teacher who possessed not one good thought about her appearance.

Twice Arthur had fallen for the heart-thumping excitement of a shallow love. But could that be called love? Or was it really the determination to possess, to have, without consideration of the many sacrifices

God expected a husband to make? Arthur had come to believe there was a very real difference in the wrong and the right way to love. If you could not lay down your own will, the determination to have your own way, love would fade away, sputter, and die.

Mary got to her feet as the silence stretched on. Arthur reached for her hand. Surprised, she jerked it away, as if she'd been stung. Real fear showed in her wide green eyes.

"Sit down."

"No, Arthur. I don't feel well at all."

"Just listen to this little bit I still have to say, then I'll go home, all right?"

Sighing, Mary sat as far away from him as possible, an elbow propped on the arm of the couch, her face held by a tightly closed fist.

"Are you listening?"

She nodded, but barely.

"I was happy being alone. I enjoyed being on the school board. The families in the community were like my own. There were a few single girls who came and went, but I felt no attraction at all. Believe me, Mary, I tried.

"When I wrote that letter to you, I simply wrote to the first person listed in the *Blackboard Bulletin* with the list of teachers in Pennsylvania. The thing I was looking for was the amount of years these young women had taught. Your twelve years were an accomplishment, I thought. Then, when I saw you digging that splinter out of your hand, I was intrigued. You were different-looking."

Mary snorted. "No doubt," she said dryly.

"No, I mean it. You were younger and much more attractive than I had planned on."

"I guess. In that dark old station."

"You have intrigued me from that first day," Arthur went on, ignoring her refusal to accept his words.

"Oddity does intrigue."

"Mary, stop it."

In answer, Mary sat up very straight. She smoothed the dark green skirt firmly over her knees that were pressed tightly together, and spoke firmly. "Arthur, I cannot accept your, your declaration of intrigue, as you call it. You know you aren't attracted to me. It's only the kindness in you, the way you pity cold, newborn calves and sick horses and dogs like Sam. You love kids and talk to old ladies and help the old men hitch up horses, and now you can add 'Boost old maids' egos' to your list of kind deeds. You know as well as I do that you do not find me attractive. Or marriageable, if you will. So save your breath. Go home and become intrigued by something else."

Arthur sighed. Then a low rumbling began in his chest, starting as a chuckle and grrowing to a full-blown guffaw of pure pleasure.

Mary turned her head sideways and watched him with suspicious eyes, and she did not smile.

Arthur finished his laugh, met her eyes, and said, "See, Mary, that is what intrigues me. Your dry sense of humor, your quick wit, and your bruising honesty. If it makes you feel any better, you are as ugly as a mud fence."

That made her laugh. She laughed quietly, sparing the vicious blisters on her lips, then said, "Hoo-eee." Very like herself. Very Mary.

Who got up first? Was it Arthur or was it Mary? Who walked the few feet first? It was as natural and as easy as if they had lived their whole lives, waiting for this moment.

His arms went around her gently, and he cradled her head on his wide, thick shoulder. That was all. They did not speak. They just stayed that way. Eventually her arms clasped his thick waist, and he sighed.

Above her head she heard Arthur say, his voice shaking with the depth of his feelings, "Thank you, Mary, for being my friend. If that's all we will ever have, I'll still cherish you as a good friend."

"Thank you, Arthur. I appreciate your friendship."

The whole way home, Arthur thought about how God worked in ordinary, mundane ways, doing what was best for his life. For what better way could have been invented than a row of miserable cold sores to keep him from placing his lips on hers? Without them, he might have declared his love to her for all time, when Mary was still on her determined path of self-hatred.

Patience, patience. This time, he'd end up with a winner, if he could only let go and let God. Indeed.

The blowing snow was beautiful but made life twice as hard, Mary decided. It drifted into every available crevice, sifting into the woodshed until it lay thickly on the split wood and melted into dirty puddles around the woodstove. If she wasn't careful, Sam would lap it up, which was disgusting. She would pounce on him immediately, scold him, and show him the water bowl—and then he tried it again. Dogs were odd creatures. Didn't he taste the sawdust?

Finally, after a week of this, she gave up and figured that if he wanted to drink melted snow with sawdust, he could. Perhaps he thought it was a fancy dish, the way the chefs gave their ordinary dishes elaborate names.

Take that picture of white bread spread with butter and sliced radishes. Mary was raised on that. It was an Amish staple in spring. *Butta brote, sals und reddich.* She'd seen a picture in *Country Living*, read the name and the recipe, then howled with laughter, kicking up her feet and bringing them down with a bang. Just look at that. Ciabatta bread, which looked like tough white bread. Butter that had a few chives in it but was still butter. Radishes sliced thin, with a bit of green stem left on, layered in decorative layers. A masterpiece. But it was still radishes and butter bread.

She even became accustomed to Sam licking up anything that fell from the countertop. Bits of bacon, a crust of bread, even a tomato or carrot or apple. She no longer bothered cleaning the floor after him. The pupils at school had informed her about the cleanliness of a dog's tongue.

Sam continued to be her guard and reliable companion. She never worried about her own safety, although she couldn't help but make some anxious searches of the distant hills at times.

She was planning her trip home for Christmas. This time she would not have to bother with Amtrak, the tickets, and the long ride alone. A van was traveling to Lancaster County, which was hard to believe, but a godsend at any rate.

Arthur told her there was a blizzard coming down from Idaho. She said she'd believe it when she saw it. He said he was worried about a few of his mother cows dropping their calves too early in the season. She didn't say it, of course, but she wanted to tell him that farmers with good management should be able to regulate that. But then, here in Montana, the cows occupied miles instead of acres, so maybe things were a little different than in tidy Lancaster County.

She considered Arthur her friend now and was so much more at ease with all this romance stuff out of the way. She figured he wasn't dumb either. Two pretty ones gone, he could keep the homely one. Well, she'd set him in his place, and she dusted her hands of any romance residue and went ahead with her life, all in the course of a week.

And then the blizzard hit.

The trees bent and swayed in its wake, creaking and groaning like suffering old men. The snow drove in, riding the powerful wind, more ice than snow, actually.

Mary staggered home from school, one hand pulling the sled, the other one held to the side of her face to avoid the stinging bits of ice. Her chest hurt from the struggle to pull the sled, but she was feeling anxious about getting home safely, the whole world turning into a vast, white, churning void that made no sense.

As usual, she was glad for Sam, who trotted ahead, his black, sturdy form reassuringly leading on. Around her, brown grasses whispered as they bent to the wind, the trees creaking and wailing from their usual positions of sturdiness.

Breathless, Mary finally reached the porch, where she had to get a shovel to dig the front door out of the tightly packed snow. When she was able to open it, she stepped through and turned to close it again but met the wind's alarming power. She struggled to shut the door.

With concern, she eyed the few pieces of wood by the fire. She couldn't admit her fear, but she dreaded opening that door again. She knew she had to. There was not enough wood to get through the night.

She almost fainted with relief when the door was yanked open and Arthur staggered in. He wasted no time in polite greetings, telling her sharply to pack some clothes. He stalked about in heavy boots, draining water pipes and turning off the refrigerator, barking orders as if she was a helpless child.

Grimly, she packed her bag, tossed in her toiletries and the book she was reading, closed it, and stood ready to go. Sam whined, begging to go. Mary snapped his leash while Arthur struggled to open the door.

Mary almost screamed with fear of the storm. She had never experienced wind of this strength. Hurricane Sandy, a year ago at home, was powerful, but this was much more frightening because of the intense cold.

Arthur was yelling, but she could not hear. He reached for her hand; she placed hers into his. The remainder of the way she tried to keep up with his large strides, but she kept foundering, slipping back down the slope. Sam lowered his head and stepped along, whining occasionally in distress.

Darkness was falling, creating an other-worldly atmosphere of whirling whiteness in a black sky as the wind slammed against their bodies, carrying their breaths away.

Arthur's house loomed out of the whirling, dizzying grayness, and Mary felt like crying with elation. The side door was away from the slamming of the wind. They fell inside and then stood, cold, breathing hard, scarcely able to grasp a place that was quiet and safe.

Slowly, Arthur unwound his scarf and pulled off his stocking cap. His mouth was still too numb to speak properly, so he motioned for Mary to go to the woodstove.

She obeyed meekly, holding out her hands to its comforting warmth. Shivering, she removed her headscarf, then her coat and sweater. She kept the black pullover on, glad for its soft warmth. Suddenly she felt ill at ease, as bashful as a schoolgirl, then chided herself. They were friends, that was all.

Arthur showed her the guest room and bathroom and told her to make herself at home, to feel free to take a hot shower, while he started supper.

She acknowledged his kindness politely. He smiled stiffly, then turned away, busying himself at the sink peeling potatoes.

He thought of cold sores, patience, and timing. He couldn't possibly have left Mary to fend for herself, and he trusted God to look out for him. But why, now, were they being thrown together like this?

Mary came into the kitchen offering to help, her face pale and frightened, the black sweater accentuating the wan circles beneath her eyes. Arthur gripped the paring knife hard and peeled potatoes with a vengeance, as he thought of holding Mary and erasing that fright from her eyes.

Politely, she inquired about the potatoes. Mashed or fried?

He was making French fries, he said. She watched from a distance as he cut the large white potatoes with an old-fashioned French fry cutter, clunking down on the handle, then dropping the oblong strips of potato in hot vegetable oil.

They were hot, greasy, and salty. A bottle of ketchup completed the meal. Arthur said they could have graham crackers and peanut butter for dessert. Dipped in milk, it was a delicious combination.

Somehow, the simple food was satisfying. It bolstered their courage as the wind struck forcefully against the large, sturdy, log house. The windows creaked as the gale mounted.

Mary helped Arthur with the dishes, stepping away self-consciously when he got too close. She often cleared her throat for something to do. He suggested a game of Monopoly, but she said no, she was too sleepy, then went off to the bathroom and had the longest shower of her life. She knew it would be more relaxing in the bathroom than in the living room with him.

She wished she would not have packed this purple robe. It was plaid and made her look like a fat hunter. She slipped the belt in the loops and backed up to the mirror to check the back view. She decided she was as wide as the bathtub, so she pulled the belt out and stuffed it in the bag.

They sat stiffly, making small talk. Arthur said the storm was expected to blow itself out in a few days, but you never could tell. She nodded. Yes, you never could tell. Mary knew if the storm lasted longer than that, she wouldn't be able to keep her friendship with him afloat without all that emotional drama connected to romance surfacing again.

She thought she had all that taken care of, finished. She should have gone to bed straightaway after her shower. Arthur complimented the robe, and she said she didn't wear it very often because it made her look like a fat hunter.

All his reserves came down, and he laughed a long relaxing laugh and told Mary they weren't handling this friendship very well. Did she think they were?

Mary said, sure they were, then lowered her eyes and kept them lowered and didn't look at him for some time.

She should not have looked at him after he got out of the shower either, with his navy blue chamois shirt and clean denim pants and bare feet. When his hair was wet, he looked so young and untroubled. The creases around his eyes made her feel as if she was having a heart attack. What did they call it? Cardiac arrest. Congestive heart failure?

He asked her why she didn't get a decent pair of ladies' slippers instead of slouching around in those men's moccasins.

Quickly, she pulled her feet in, sliding her heels up the footrest of the recliner. She said clearly, "My feet are as big as flippers."

Arthur looked at Mary for a long time. He said he'd never noticed.

Well, they were a 9 ½, sometimes 10, so she may as well slap around in flippers.

She went to bed, then, when he didn't laugh. She knelt by her bed and asked God to please give her strength to be friends with Arthur and nothing more.

If the only way out of this quagmire of feelings was to go home, then please let the van leave for Pennsylvania a week early. Otherwise, she was afraid she couldn't manage this business with Arthur with any real sense of truthfulness.

Arthur lay in his bed, shaking and laughing, thinking how she said she looked like a fat hunter in that bathrobe.

Chapter Ten

I<small>N THE MORNING, THE ONLY LIGHT THAT FOUND</small> its way through the slight crack between the curtains was gray, dull, and not very effective in waking anyone, so it was past eight o'clock when Mary's eyes flew open, startled. The small black alarm clock gave away the fact that she had overslept terribly.

Leaping from the bed, she dressed hurriedly and brushed her teeth. Then she combed her red hair, pinned the covering neatly over it, tied on her black big apron, and opened the bathroom door slowly.

The house was empty. Through the wide, high windows in the seating area she could see a world of whirling, churning, blowing snow. The wind had abated somewhat so that the windows no longer made that frightening, popping sound of the night before. Still a sizable storm, she thought.

The house was warm, as a bright wood fire crackled and popped behind the glass in the door of the large woodstove. Steam rose from the blue granite coffee pot on the top.

Mary inhaled deeply. Had Arthur been up for awhile? He'd made coffee already. Quietly, as if she might waken him, Mary tiptoed to the kitchen and opened the pine doors of the top cupboards, searching for cups or mugs.

She smiled to herself when she found the largest, heaviest mugs she'd ever seen, the insignia of a bear imprinted on both sides. Hmm. Very masculine, Arthur.

She drank her coffee black, liking it piping hot. This was perfect coffee. She wrapped her thin fingers gratefully around the gigantic cup, stood by the woodstove, and surveyed Arthur's house. Log walls, deer horns, elk horns, wildlife pictures, a brown leather sofa and chairs. Rugs that came straight from some mail order catalog that catered to the rugged life.

She thought of her things. The impossibility of joining the two tastes, her things soft and flowery and so Lancaster County. Two different worlds.

She saw the papers thrown on top of the kitchen table, the pens in the wooden holder, some loose change, a retractable utility knife. This was a man's world, and her things would be out of place. It felt incongruous to even think about it. Still she did.

When the door was pulled open and Arthur stumbled through it, covered with snow, Mary looked up, not quite sure what she should say, if she should speak at all. Quickly, she lifted her cup, taking a scalding sip.

"Good morning, Mary! I hope you slept well," Arthur said, in a brisk, booming voice.

She nodded, watching warily as he pulled off his stocking cap, rid himself of the heavy coat in one fast shrug, then bent to loosen his boots.

Without further words, he got down a mug, poured it full of coffee, took a sip, and smiled down at her. "Good morning, Mary," he said as softly as he could.

See? That was the first mistake of the day, Mary thought. If she would have kept her eyes on the storm or the coffee pot or any other trustworthy place, her heart would not have kicked up its rhythm. When that happened, all the unwanted drama came tumbling along. That thing people called romance.

As it was, she lost herself in the new and startling gentleness in the blue glints that were his eyes, half buried in those attractive creases that gave away the goodness of his character. She felt herself hurtling through space, as she may as well have been. She had to get her feet back on solid ground, then glue them firmly with the Super Glue called reality.

To do that, she had to stop looking at him, or at least his eyes. Eyes were tricky. You had to be careful. How many times had she taken glints of humor, friendliness, laughter, or a look that lasted a few seconds longer than necessary, as meaning the young man was interested in her? Too many times to count.

Mary stepped away from him, sliding her feet softly to the left out of the circle that wasn't safe. She watched the storm, then looked at the head of an elk, its horns as big as anything she had ever seen.

Finally, Arthur spoke. "Are you interested in accompanying me today?"

"Doing what?" Mary spoke to the elk antlers. They were much safer.

"Do you ride?"

"No. I never did."

"Not too late to learn."

She shook her head.

"I need to find a few cows. I think about half a dozen are missing. I'm especially worried about the one who should be about ready to calf."

"I'll stay here."

"You sure?"

Mary looked at the whirling snow. She thought of riding a horse through it. She'd be going home for Christmas to stay and would not be back, so why not? Why pass up an opportunity like this? It was a once in a lifetime experience. One she would tell her friend Sarah Fisher, stringing it out, embellishing it like too many Christmas lights on one tree. They'd shriek and laugh at her clumsiness. Life would return to normal as soon as she went home for Christmas.

First, Arthur made pancakes, the biggest, thickest pancakes Mary had ever seen. The two-burner griddle held only two, so they really were the size of dinner plates.

She watched as he flipped them onto a plate, melted at least two tablespoons of butter across them, added maple syrup, added another layer of pancakes, and then repeated the procedure again.

He cooked sausages, thin wide patties of browned sausage that tasted so good, Mary ate two. But she could not eat all those huge pancakes. Besides, she was not used to maple syrup. It was too thin and too sweet with an odd, sharp flavor. She was used to Aunt Jemima's syrup. Or Country Kitchen. Or anything Walmart had on special. But, of course, she didn't say that.

Not once did Mary meet Arthur's eyes, which was good. She did the dishes alone, which was good, too. At least he wasn't too close. It was much easier to keep her little boat called *No Romance* afloat if she stayed clear of his eyes or presence.

She dressed warmly, putting on her black jersey pants, those fleece-lined, cumbersome, unattractive, necessary things she wore beneath her skirts to walk to school. Then she added two sweaters, a heavy black coat, a scarf, and a headscarf on her head, a pair of study boots, and her thick gloves.

Arthur remained strangely quiet as they dressed, but Mary figured he was busy and thought nothing of it. Together they floundered through the blowing snow, eventually falling through the heavy barn door, panting.

Arthur immediately set to work saddling the horses. "This one is named Tessa. I call her Tess. She's a quarter horse, small, surefooted, and so safe a five-year-old could ride her. She follows my horse around wherever he goes, so all you have to do is sit in the saddle, and she'll follow, okay?"

Mary nodded. She liked the looks of the small brown horse. She was compact with a gentle look in her brown eyes, a softness about her that instantly endeared her to Mary's heart. She stroked the side of her neck, rubbed the velvety nose. She was used to horses; she had been around them all her life. Her own driving horse, Ginger, was a high-stepping sad-dlebred who obeyed Mary completely.

Arthur came to stand beside her. Mary moved away.

"She likes you," he said softly.

"Looks like it."

"Good. I'm glad. You'll do fine. You need help up?"

Mary looked at the saddle, then at the height of the stirrup. She made the huge mistake of forgetting herself and looking at Arthur with a timid unguard-ed question in her eyes, completely uncharacteristic and too vulnerable. Whoa. Her boat of *No Romance* was tilted by a wave that crashed out of nowhere. Mary's eyes slid away and she lifted her chin. The boat righted itself and went steadfastly on its way. Good.

Grasping the saddle horn, she inserted the toe of her boot into the stirrup, hopped up and down a few times, and flung herself into the saddle. She almost slid down the other side, but instead, righted herself and sat solidly, getting used to the feel of the saddle. She had never seen a horse from this spot. The ground seemed so far away, the horse's ears and mane too long and too far below her. She felt clumsy, as if she weighed twice as much as usual. Lifting her shoulders, she straightened her back. She did know enough about riding to understand that slouching or sagging in the saddle was very unattractive.

Arthur tightened the cinch around the stomach of his own horse, then turned to look at her and smiled. "You sit a horse very well."

"Thanks."

"You really do, Mary."

Arthur opened the wide, heavy barn door, and Tessa turned obediently when Mary lifted the reins.

She stepped out into the storm, her ears flicking forward, then back. After that, she lowered her head and bent to the task of following Arthur's horse.

Sam whined from the barn, but the sound was soon lost in the wind. He had to stay, of course. The snow came up to the horses' undersides in places.

Mary loved the snow. She had always enjoyed winter, watching motorists on Route 30 creep along, their windshield wipers moving back and forth furiously, the drivers peering anxiously from behind wet glass, honking horns, sliding into ditches. She loved the power of the great yellow trucks from "the state," as Dat said, their chains clanking, their immense blades shoving the cinders and salt and gray slush in a precise arc along the side of the road. Neighbors shoveled snow, called greetings to each other, spread salt on doorsteps. That was Mary's Lancaster County winters, the snow mixed with lights, black telephone poles, moving cars and buggies, and people.

Here in this moment, the solitude was awe-inspiring. Mary had never known you could actually hear snow fall. It whispered. It sang a haunting, beautiful melody as it rode the gale, as if some of God's angels wrote the song of the snow and God directed the symphony of nature from His throne.

The pine trees' movement rid them of their heavy layer of snow before it had a chance to settle. They looked black, so dark was the green, bent and swaying like restless dancers, tossed about. An occasional pine cone socked into the ever deepening snow with a barely audible sound.

Downhill was frightening. Mary fought the desire to grasp the saddle horn with both hands. Better to find the balance she needed with the stirrups supporting her weight.

Tess stopped, her nose very close to Arthur's horse's rump. He turned.

"You okay?' he shouted.

"Yes."

"You sure?"

"Yes."

"We'll be going uphill for while. There's a grove of trees over the next rise. Sometimes, cattle will take shelter there."

"Okay." Mary's voice was flung from her, carried away by the wind.

They rode up a long slope, then down the opposite side, where they located a group of five cows huddled beneath a group of bare, swaying trees. Mary saw the reason they had stayed behind. Two small calves were half buried in the drifting snow. The mothers mooed with a high shrill sound of anxiety, the wail of nature, willing their offspring to live.

For as bulky as Arthur was, he was off his horse in one swift movement. Mary remained in the saddle, watching, as he bent to check for signs of life. He straightened, looked at his horse, then back at Mary.

"They're both alive," he shouted.

Mary didn't answer him, knowing it was useless. She was beginning to feel the cold penetrating her outerwear. A shiver chased itself up her back. Her teeth began to chatter.

She reached up and pulled the woolen scarf across her mouth so Arthur wouldn't see. "I can take one on my saddle."

Arthur looked at Mary, questioning.

She nodded. "I can try," she shouted.

His horse stood perfectly still as Arthur bent to the task of tying the small hooves together, the mother

cows anxiously mooing. Through the whirling whiteness he appeared, his arms cupped around the helpless calf. Suddenly a solid thump of brown weight
was thrown across her lap, followed by his voice.

"You sure?"

Mary wasn't one bit sure. She was cold and shivering now. The calf smelled wet and sour. She looked
down at the thick, matted hair, the terrified, bulging
eyes of the just-born calf, and wanted to tell Arthur
to take it. It smelled and would very likely die of cold
and exposure, and then she would feel responsible.
Grimly, she watched the limp tail and hoped with all
her heart it would not lift and expel the unthinkable
all over her lap.

"Ready?"

In answer, Mary lifted a gloved hand in a forward
motion. Arthur sprang to his horse, settled himself in
the saddle, turned, and started off. Tess followed immediately. Bawling incessantly, the five cows trotted
beside them, falling back when they slipped, trotting,
floundering, then settling into a steady walk, their
heads bobbing rhythmically the way Holsteins did
when they walked.

Mary remembered the farm well. She always brought in the cows, using Doddy Stoltzfus's walking cane, shouting "Hoos-sa! Hoos-sa!" The language of five generations of Stoltzfuses, Dat said. She fed calves, washed milkers, and washed the cows' teats before attaching the heavy, gleaming milking machines.

But it had been a while. Dat and Mam had moved off the farm and retired to the small ranch house along Route 30. Jonas had taken over the farm, and Mary forgot the scent of newborn calves, the bawling of anxious mothers.

Never once in her wildest dreams would she have imagined being in this faraway place, following this man through a storm of this size. God moved in mysterious ways, she thought, omitting the rest of the verse—"His wonders to perform."

Huh. No wonders for this old maid. Everything was still under control. The storm would wear thin, the clouds would open up, the blue would show in the west, and the sun would break through again. She would leave Arthur's house and go home for two weeks. She'd board the van, the long, fifteen-passenger vehicle, that would travel the 1,800 miles home to Lancaster County to resume her normal life.

She watched the sky anxiously now, dreading any sign of the storm thinning out. She wanted the snow to keep whirling out of gray skies; she wanted the wind to keep whining and howling around the barn and the house. She dreaded the blue of the clear sky, plowing the roads, the sun's warmth. With all her heart, she wanted to stay here.

Lifting her shoulders, she swiped viciously at her nose, then squeezed her eyes shut at the pain. Ouch. She likely had a frostbitten appendage now for sure.

Well, what you wanted and what you got were two completely different things usually, and this was no different. Older, she was now, and wiser. Yes, she wanted to stay, but coupled with that knowledge came the realization of the disappointment that was sure to follow. You could easily shoulder disappointment. She'd often done it. It wasn't hard after a while.

The calf slung across the saddle struggled weakly. Mary placed a gloved hand across its back, pressed down and said, "You're okay, there." She took a deep breath, straightening her back. Her legs were

beginning to ache. A fine layer of snow that had settled on her scarf began to melt and drain down her
back, sending goose bumps up and down her arms.

The mother cow jostled against Mary's booted
foot, knocking it out of the stirrup. Mary reinserted
her foot, kicked out at the anxious, bawling creature,
then righted herself and kept riding. It seemed an
eternity until the dark barn loomed through the gray,
whirling world.

Mary heard Sam whine anxiously before Arthur
dismounted and flung the barn doors wide, allowing
Mary to ride through. He closed them behind her,
leaving the cows behind as he latched it. He worked
quickly, pulling the calves down, rubbing them with
an old feedsack. He massaged their chests and listened to both calves' hearts before asking Mary to go
to the house for hot water.

She was barely able to stand, let alone walk to the
house. She tottered off grimly without looking back,
wishing she had Doddy Stoltzfus's cane.

Sam leaped and whined beside her, cavorting in
the snow, spending his pent-up energy in senseless
hops and circles of needless tail-catching.

Mary plodded up the slope as if her feet were encased in blocks of ice. They felt worse than flippers now.

She returned with steaming hot water in the lidded pail Arthur had provided. Without a word of thanks, he took it from her brusquely. She stood beside him, her too-long arms with the too-big hands covered with freckles and hanging by her sides.

She watched as he mixed the yellowish powder into the bucket, his eyes squinted in concentration. When he was satisfied with the dissolved powder, he poured a portion of the liquid into a plastic bottle, then another.

When he didn't ask for her assistance, Mary leaned against the rough lumber of the box stall.

Arthur lifted the calf's nose, attempting to get it to suckle the rubber nipple, but nothing happened. The calf's head flopped into the straw. Frustrated, he tried the second calf with the same result. He must not know much about calves, Mary thought. And, if he didn't ask, she wouldn't offer. She was surprised when he sat back on his heels, shook his head, and said they'd likely not make it.

"Sure they will," Mary answered quickly.

Forgetting herself and thinking only of the calves, Mary unscrewed the cap of the bottle, placed the rubber nipple in the proper position, and tightened the ring. She inserted two fingers into the one calf's mouth and pried its jaw open. Then she quickly stuck the nipple in and let the newborn have a go at it.

She was rewarded by a licking of a soft pink tongue. She repeated the maneuver with the other calf, the way she used to as a child, until both calves were on their feet, working away at their bottles with wet, smacking sounds, the excess running out of the corners of their mouths.

Arthur watched, his eyes shining. "Hearty little orphans, aren't they?" he said, finally.

"They're not orphans," Mary corrected him.

"The mothers probably won't take them now."

"Holsteins would."

"How do you know so much about cows?"

"The farm."

"Mmm."

Arthur watched Mary while she washed the bottles with the hose in the water trough. He fed the horses, threw hay to the five cows that had returned late, and said he was cold.

When they trudged silently to the house and he strode ahead of her without speaking, she didn't let it bother her. She had to start working on accepting the end of the storm and the end of her time at Arthur's house, so she may as well begin now. She had displeased him somehow, but that was all right. If he remained in a quiet, unresponsive mood, it would make her leaving even lighter.

So when the snow thinned out, the wind died down, and the blue sky appeared, Mary was fully prepared. She went to the guest room, folded the plaid robe, found her slippers, and put everything efficiently into the Coach bag, the small one, and thought how nice it would be to go shopping again.

Arthur offered her lunch, but she declined politely, speaking to the coffee pot this time. She pulled on her boots, buttoned her coat, tied her scarf and said, "Thank you for everything, Arthur" in one hurried, flat sentence, opened the door, and let herself out.

She walked all alone, plowing resolutely through the deepening drifts, Sam bouncing and yipping energetically beside her.

Arthur stood at the big windows, watching the stoic figure that was Mary, until she disappeared behind the line of trees close to her house. He did not turn away until he saw a dark plume of smoke begin to come up out of the chimney and swirl away into the white world. She'd figure out how to turn the water system back on, he supposed. She was capable.

He had exactly two weeks left and positively no idea how to convince her that he wanted her, that he needed her to stay. Somehow he doubted his ability to persuade her of this fact.

Chapter Eleven

STRAINS OF CHRISTMAS CAROLS ROSE AND FELL IN the schoolhouse the last evening that Mary would be in Montana. The tinsel glistened in the propane light, the red and green ribbons, drawn to the center of the ceiling from each corner, turned and twisted slightly from the movement below. Homemade, white snowflakes hung from the ceiling as well, with red and white candy canes promenading across the lower half of the windows.

The children were dressed in red and green, their faces shining in the lamplight as they sang. "God rest ye merry, gentlemen, let nothing you dismay, for Jesus Christ our Savior, was born this Christmas Day."

The parents were in awe of the singing. Their own children singing like this was unimaginable. They had never heard these songs. When they launched into a tender version of "What Child Is This?", mothers wept discreetly into their babies' burp cloths, blinked, blew their noses, and felt a bit ashamed. When the schoolchildren formed a large circle and held hands while singing the old hymn, "Bind Us Together," they gave up and cried.

"Bind us together, Lord, bind us together, Lord, bind us together with love."

Mary was going home to stay. She told the community they would find someone to finish the school year. She felt like a quitter but not a failure. She had not failed at her teaching. She had been a success, as she knew she would be. Tonight it hurt worse than she could have imagined though, the parting so painful it made her feel oblivious to everything. While others cried, she remained stone-faced.

No one needed to know why she was going home. They all ate the Christmas meal, exchanged and shared pleasantries back and forth. For Mary, the evening was mechanical, robotic, as if she was programmed to get through this last night together. She hugged mothers, shook fathers' hands, clasped the children to her heart, and told them she'd always remember them her whole life. They'd write. She'd write back. They'd visit someday.

Empty promises, she knew, but promises. The kind that made parting bearable.

Alone, she swept the floor and burned the trash. How many offers had she declined? But Arthur had not offered at all. So there. She had been right. He would forget about her the minute she was in that van headed for Pennsylvania.

Smart. Everything under control, easily managed. Tomorrow, her journey home. The day after that, she'd be at home in time for Christmas.

Her LED lamp bobbed beside her as Sam trotted obediently by the sled she pulled with gloved hands. Every star in the vast, black sky blinked down at her as if they wanted to remind her of her last night here in God's great sky country. She lifted her face, savoring the still, cold air, the light of the friendly stars, the sliver of moon that kept her company.

When she reached her house, she carried the boxes of presents inside, then set the sled carefully against the wall. Absentmindedly, she wondered why Arthur had never finished this ugly old porch with the twisted posts.

No problem now. Perhaps in the spring he would. She packed her presents, preparing to have them sent by UPS with the remainder of her things. She unfolded her last paycheck, gasped at the large bonus, then blinked. Finally, in the shelter of her own house, away from eyes that asked questions, one round tear hung on her lashes, quivered and splashed on the cardboard box she was closing with packing tape. She swiped blindly at the wetness, despising her own weakness. She honked into a clean tissue, threw it into the waste can hard, leaving the lid swinging back and forth.

Arthur would be here in the morning for Sam. He was his dog. She tried not to look at him too much, the way he lay beside the woodstove with his head on his paws, neatly, like a folded towel or a book replaced on a shelf. His eyes watched every movement, as if he knew she would be leaving.

Mary showered, then checked the clock. Eleven-thirty. She'd have to get up early, by at least five o'clock if the van was picking her up at seven.

She was hungry, so she poured the last of her Raisin Bran into a bowl, added milk and sugar, and leaned against the counter to eat it. After a few bites, she gave up and set it beside the sink. She had had to choke down the Christmas dinner at school, and she'd managed only a few bites before sliding her plate into the garbage, still half-filled.

She blew out the one lone Christmas candle on the table, then turned to twist the knob of the propane gas lamp, when she froze. A knock?

Who could be at her door this late at night? Should she open it?

For the hundredth time she wished she had a door with a window in it, but since that was not the case, she had two choices. One, open the door and face the consequences. Two, leave the door shut and crawl under the bed and face the same consequences.

If someone meant her harm, they'd break in anyway, Mam always said. In a way, it was logical, but to open the door wide, facing danger head on, was just plain stupid. So she did nothing.

She dug a piece of Raisin Bran cereal out of her teeth with the toothpick she was holding and waited. She didn't know why she waited, but it was the only safe thing to do. When the knob turned from outside, and the door was pushed slowly inward, Mary froze.

As still as if she'd been made of granite, she kept her eyes on the door, watching the ever widening distance between the door and the frame. It was filled with black. No stars or porch roof were visible. When Arthur's voice filled the black space, saying her name softly with a question mark behind it, Mary's knees wobbled. She sank to a chair, grateful for its support.

"Come in," she called.

She had never been so glad to see him. There were plenty of times when she had been happy at the sight of him, but not with this relief, this sudden realization that nothing bad was going to happen to her.

"Mary?"

"What on earth, Arthur?"

"Mary, listen."

She was prepared to have him tell her he'd come to get Sam. Or anything else. She had not prepared herself for this haggard, shaking version of the man she knew so well.

"You can't leave," he burst out.

Mary was speechless.

"You can't go back," Arthur repeated, thickly.

"But . . ."

"For once, Mary, be quiet and listen. I don't know how to get this across. You have to believe me this time. I don't want you to go home. I want you to stay here. Not here, in this house. I mean . . ." His voice trailed off and he shook his head. Mary had never seen him so miserable. The poor man was in a bad way.

"I'm getting this all wrong."

Mary watched his face, surprised that she could not say a word of contradiction or denial.

Finally, he sagged in defeat. He simply walked over to her where she sat white-faced in the kitchen chair. He looked down at her and said, so soft and low it was only a rough whisper, "I love you, Mary."

He pulled her to her feet. She probably would not have been able to stand except that she was crushed against him by his strong arms coming around her.

"I can't get the words right," he said gently. He bent his head, found her mouth with some difficulty, and let his kiss speak the language of the universe, a sweet sense of possession, a conveyance of love and need.

Mary had never been kissed. She had never been held like this. All the usual denial, the normal resistance, was banished in that space of time. The little boat called *No Romance* sank immediately to the ocean floor, replaced by a white ship with every sail unfolded, accompanied by songs of love, bright lights of acknowledgment and acceptance, happiness and joy and gratitude.

Later, while his arms held Mary, Arthur found his voice, although it was hampered by small chokes of emotion. "Mary, will you stay? Will you promise to stay a while longer? At least till I gather enough courage to ask you to be my wife?"

At the word "wife," Mary drew back in alarm. "I am not a wife. I am an old maid."

"But can't old maids turn into wives?" Arthur asked.

Mary shrugged her shoulders. "I don't know," she said, completely puzzled.

As Arthur remained seated on the sofa, his arms fell away. Suddenly his whole body began to shake, his face turned red, and he burst into a long, musical wave of laughter that was so infectious Mary began to laugh quietly, then erupted into a full howl of ungraceful mirth that matched his.

He said her name three times and gathered her back into the circle of his arms, where she stayed until he released her. He slid down on one knee and took her hand.

"My dear, old maid Mary, will you be my wife?" he said, very soft and low, like a benediction.

Mary looked down at her long, thin fingers on the long, thin hand with freckles on the back of it, nestled in Arthur's thick, heavy hands. It looked exactly right. Her hands were beautiful, graceful, perfect.

She whispered, "Yes, Arthur. I will be your wife."

"Thank you, Mary," he said, as reverently as he felt.

Sam watched from his bed by the stove, blinked a few times, then went back to sleep. The fire in the woodstove burned down to embers. Mary said she didn't know what she'd do about going home for Christmas, suddenly becoming subdued and a little worried.

Arthur said the choice was hers. She could go if she wanted.

Mary's eyes never left his face. She etched every crease in her mind, folding them away in her heart. His eyes spoke the word "home." Arthur was her home. He was the haven for her bruised heart. How long had she fought her own heart?

"Arthur, I have come home for Christmas. Wherever you are, that is where I belong. I'll see my family at the . . . the . . ." Stammering, suddenly unsure if she should actually speak the word, "wedding," Mary stopped, which started Arthur chuckling happily all over again.

Their wedding was in the spring on a sunny April day that was freshly showered by fine rain. Every new leaf was washed by dewdrops, warmed by a sun holding the promise of summer.

The farm had been prepared by her frenzied family, for Mary's announcement had set them all properly on their heads with astonishment. Her sisters shrieked and held their hands to their cheeks, their eyes bulging. Her brothers laughed softly and said, "Leave it to Mary to go gallivanting off to wild

Montana and return with a husband in tow, then, yet, one named 'Arthur Bontrager.'"

But when they actually met Arthur, they liked him immediately. They followed him around wherever he went, slapping their knees with laughter at his Western-accented stories. They put their heads together and decided that Mary had caught herself a very nice guy after all those years of spinsterhood.

When Mary stood in front of Bishop Joel Blank, her hand was placed in Arthur's, and the blessing followed. She had repeated her two "*Yas*" of promise, and she could truthfully say it was every bit as wonderful as she had always imagined.

Her teaching career was over after that term, of course. She moved into Arthur's house with him, and one of the first things she did was wash windows, scour, and clean the place, saying it was clean enough for a man, but certainly not for a woman.

She could wear worn, old handkerchiefs over her hair that was not carefully combed, look in the mirror, and smile. It was a wonder. She was freed of all that useless, heavy baggage called "disliking oneself," a polite version of hating almost everything about your looks. She saw herself through Arthur's eyes now. He told her over and over how beauty is in the eye of the beholder, and that God does not want us to bury ourselves in piles of insecurity.

She washed clothes in the Maytag wringer washer and hung them on the line in the summer breezes that never stopped. She cooked and baked, her feet treading lightly on clouds of contentment. And some days, she merely sat, steeped in happiness, like fine tea that improves the longer it steeps.

She had been happy before because of the school-children. She had been supremely blessed; not one year had been empty or wasted, and for that she was grateful. She knew, too, that for someone like her to be given a person like Arthur surpassed understanding. She was not worthy. He was a gift.

When their daughter was born, they named her Leah, for Mary's aging grandmother. Leah was a gift, too. Mary had never imagined having children. It would be asking too much from God, after He'd provided her with such a fine husband.

She felt a deep sadness whenever the fast-paced younger generation got married, had children, and then marriage problems surfaced. Was it really the fault of these beautiful young creatures? Maybe they had never given up hope of a happy marriage. They ran around and dated lots, not thinking about the blessings and sacrifices that are part of being married. They didn't expect struggles or hardships. Maybe they were too young. Perhaps, but who knew?

Mary watched Leah toddling across the green grass under the great blue Montana sky, and she thanked God for her little girl, her wonderful Arthur, and even for her freckles and red hair.

They were all truly a blessing.

The End

More Books by Linda Byler

Available from your favorite bookstore or online retailer.

"Author Linda Byler is Amish, which sets this book apart
both in the rich details of Amish life and in the lack of melo-
drama over disappointments and tragedies. Byler's writing
will leave readers eager for the next book in the series."
— *Publishers Weekly*

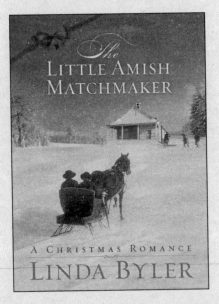

THE LITTLE AMISH MATCHMAKER
A Christmas Romance

LIZZIE SEARCHES FOR LOVE SERIES

BOOK ONE   BOOK TWO   BOOK THREE

TRILOGY   COOKBOOK

SADIE'S MONTANA SERIES

BOOK ONE   BOOK TWO   BOOK THREE   TRILOGY

LANCASTER BURNING SERIES

BOOK ONE   BOOK TWO   BOOK THREE

About the Author

Linda Byler was raised in an Amish family and is an active member of the Amish church today. Growing up, Linda loved to read and write. In fact, she still does. Linda is well-known within the Amish community as a columnist for a weekly Amish newspaper.

Linda is the author of the *Lizzie Searches for Love* series, the *Sadie's Montana* series, the *Lancaster Burning* series, and the *Hester's Hunt for Home* series, featuring a Native American child who is raised by an Amish family in colonial America. The first novel in that series is *Hester on the Run*.

Linda is also the author of *The Little Amish Matchmaker* and *The Christmas Visitor*, two Christmas romances. She is author, too, of *Lizzie's Amish Cookbook: Favorite recipes from three generations of Amish cooks!*